Pre
The We

CW00801234

'I loved this story of two best fri...,
the excitement and tensions of World War Two. Sarah Webb has not only
brilliantly captured life during the Emergency, but the dynamics of friendship
between two very different girls. A gripping adventure and a great read!'
Marita Conlon-McKenna, author of *Under the Hawthorn Tree* and *Fairy Hill*

'A wartime tale with a difference. A magnificent setting on the west coast
of Ireland. A beautiful story that celebrates courage, resilience and
most of all – friendship.' Patricia Forde, Laureate na nÓg (2023-2026)

'I loved this book so much. I read it in one sitting and immediately wanted
to start over again. Sarah writes with such warmth and kindness towards her
characters – they feel like old friends. Sarah is a natural born storyteller and I'd
highly recommend this book for young (and not so young) readers.'
Judi Curtin, author of the *Alice and Megan* and *Lily at Lissadell* series

Praise for Sarah Webb's other books

'Sarah Webb has yet again delivered a fantastic adventure of change, family,
and friendship.' *Books Ireland* on *The Little Bee Charmer of Henrietta Street*

'This is the book for every little girl who dreams of changing the world.'
Irish Independent on *Blazing a Trail*

'Webb's book could be just the thing to provide encouragement that someone,
regardless of age, might need to believe in themselves and realise that there
is no dream that is too big.'
Irish Examiner on *Be Inspired!*

For more information on the author and her books, visit obrien.ie

Dedication

The Weather Girls is dedicated to the memory of Maureen Sweeney (née Flavin), the remarkable woman who inspired this story. 1923-2023

First published 2024 by The O'Brien Press Ltd,
12 Terenure Road East, Rathgar, Dublin 6, D06 HD27, Ireland.
Tel: +353 1 4923333; Fax: +353 1 4922777
E-mail: books@obrien.ie; Website: obrien.ie
The O'Brien Press is a member of Publishing Ireland.

ISBN: 978-1-78849-439-7

1 3 5 7 8 6 4 2
24 26 28 27 25

Printed and bound in Great Britain by Clays Ltd, Elcograf S.p.A.
The paper in this book is produced using pulp from managed forests

The Weather Girls receives financial assistance from the Arts Council.

Sarah Webb wishes to thank the Arts Council for the Literature Bursary that allowed her to research and write this book.

Published in

DUBLIN

UNESCO
City of Literature

The
Weather
Girls

SARAH WEBB

THE O'BRIEN PRESS
DUBLIN

World War Two

World War Two was a terrible conflict that involved most of the countries in the world. It began because the leader of Germany, a man called Adolf Hitler, wanted to expand German territory. He decided to do this by invading other countries, starting with Poland.

There were two sides in the war, the Axis (including Germany, Japan and Italy) and the Allies (Britain, the US and others). Millions of people were killed during the war. It started in September 1939 and ended in September 1945: six long years.

Ireland, like many other countries, remained neutral during the war. The Taoiseach at the time, Éamon de Valera, brought in emergency laws to run the country, so the period became known as 'The Emergency'. However, as you'll find out in *The Weather Girls*, many people in Ireland secretly helped the Allies.

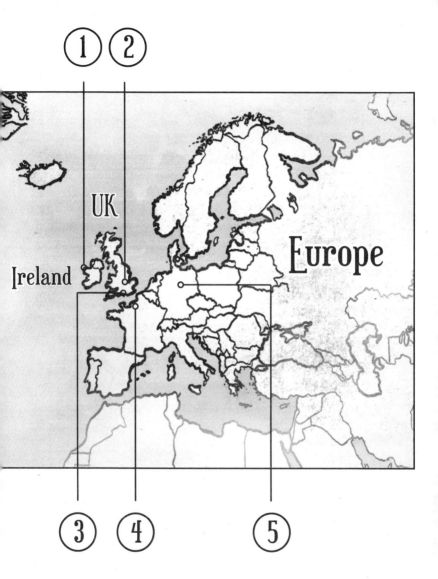

1. Blacksod, Mayo
2. Dunstable, UK
3. Portsmouth, UK
4. Normandy, France
5. Germany

Weather Instruments

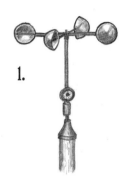

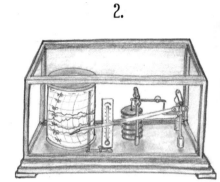

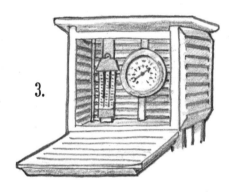

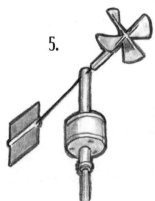

1. Anemometer
2. Barometer
3. Thermometer in Stevenson screen
4. Rain gauge
5. Wind vane

PROLOGUE

Saturday 14th June, 1941

'One day I'll be up there.' Sibby points at the red velvet curtains in front of us. We're sitting beside each other in the picture house at Claremorris. 'A matinee star, like Maureen O'Hara. She's Irish, you know.'

I put on my best radio presenter voice, all deep and dramatic, and say, 'Maureen was whisked away to Hollywood at eighteen to star in *The Hunchback of Notre Dame* and has never looked back.'

Sibby stares at me. 'How do you know all that?'

'You've only told me her story a hundred times,' I reply. 'You're obsessed with Maureen O'Hara.'

Sibby grins. 'She deserves attention. She's so glamorous. Like me.' She frames her head with her hands and pouts.

I laugh. 'Just like you.'

There's a mechanical click and the curtains start to open for the Pathé news – a black-and-white newsreel that comes on before the main picture.

'Girls, are you ready?' Mamó says. 'The reel's starting.' Her eyes are glued to the big screen. Mamó seems just as excited to be at the pictures as I am.

Mamó is Sibby's grandmother. She drove us to Claremorris today to see the film *Dumbo* as a special treat. Sibby loves the picture house, and she's been loads of times. It's only my second time after seeing *Pinocchio* last year – again with Sibby and Mamó – so it's pretty special for me.

'I'll be on all the newsreels one day,' Sibby says. 'Grace, say something like "Mayo actress takes over the world" in your funny accent.'

I deepen my voice again. 'Miss Elizabeth Lavelle, Mayo's answer to Maureen O'Hara, takes the silver screen by storm.' Elizabeth is Sibby's real name. No-one calls her that, but she says it's going to be her 'stage name' one day.

Sibby beams with delight. 'Ha! "Mayo's answer to Maureen O'Hara"! I love it!'

Someone behind us tut-tuts. Sibby grins and rolls her eyes. 'One day grown-ups will appreciate our tremendous talent and outstanding wit,' she says as the screen crackles into life and the newsreel comes on. Everyone in the picture house starts to clap and whistle.

'They will,' I say over the noise. 'But maybe not today.'

Sibby nudges me with her shoulder. 'Happy birthday, Grace. Hope you like your picture house trip.'

'Best present ever,' I say. 'Thanks, kindred spirit.'

This is what my favourite book character, Anne of Green Gables, calls her best friend. I loved the book so much I made Sibby read it too. She liked it, but she didn't *love* it. Not enough drama, apparently. Which is nonsense – it's full of drama!

Sibby laughs. 'You're welcome,' she says.

A posh male voice booms out through the speakers. 'This is the Pathé Newsreel for June 1941. Belfast is still in shock from the recent bombings which killed over a thousand innocent civilians.'

The screen is filled with German planes flying over Belfast and dropping bombs. There are loud explosions and then burning buildings, blown up bridges, children running away from the blasts, screaming. The images are so vivid I can almost taste smoke and dust in my mouth. My heart squeezes. It's horrible!

Beside me I can hear Mamó say, 'Poor souls.'

The newsreel continues. 'On Burke Street, all twenty houses were wiped off the map. Here we see Dublin firemen fighting the blaze. De Valera himself sent thirteen Irish fire tenders to help deal with the fires that raged all over the great city.'

As we watch, fireman struggle with thick hoses, trying to drench the towering flames.

'Who's De Valera again?' Sibby asks me.

'Sibby!' I say. 'He's our Taoiseach.'

'Oh yes, I remember now,' she says. 'But why is he sending fire engines to Belfast? I thought we were supposed to be neutral?'

Someone behind us coughs loudly, and another person gives a loud 'shush'.

'Girls, you're disturbing people,' Mamó says. 'Hush now. Watch the newsreel.'

My cheeks flare up, but it's dark so no one can see them. 'Sorry, Mamó,' I whisper.

Beside me, Sibby chuckles behind her hand. She's not as bothered about what other people think as I am. Sometimes I wish I could be more like her.

As I continue to stare at the burning buildings on the screen, the tops of my hands tingle and I start to feel a bit sick. Hitler bombed Dublin in January too. What if he bombs Blacksod next? I know it's unlikely – so far, it's mainly been cities, and why would he attack our small Mayo village? – but I can't stop thinking about it. I take a deep breath and try to calm my nerves. *Hitler is not interested in Blacksod*, Grace, I tell myself. *Get a grip!*

The newsreel comes to an end, and jaunty circus music plays as the credits for *Dumbo* start to roll. *Da-da, diddly, da-da, daaa-da.*

'Dumbo!' Sibby jumps up and down in her seat. 'And look, a circus tent!'

The woman behind us sighs loudly. 'Here, are you going to gasp and talk the whole way through the picture?' she asks Sibby.

Sibby swings around, bold as anything. 'I'm sorry, I'm a very emotional person,' she says. 'I just can't help myself. I might gasp, but it won't be on purpose. But I do promise not to talk.'

Luckily the woman finds this funny. She chuckles. 'Ah, sure, I'm a bit of a chatterbox myself. Do your best, love.'

'I will,' Sibby says. 'I promise.'

And I do *my* best to concentrate on *Dumbo* and to forget about the blazing buildings I've just seen. Cute cartoon baby animals are being flown through the sky to their mothers, carefully held in the mouths of storks. Forget about Belfast, I tell myself. Think about the circus and the baby animals!

* * *

In the car on the way home, Sibby is still teary. 'It was so tragic,' she says, giving a dramatic sigh. 'Poor little Dumbo. But at least it had a happy ending. Did you like it, Grace?'

I nod. 'I loved it. Apart from the newsreel. I didn't know that many people had died in Belfast.'

'I hope it didn't upset you too much, Grace,' Mamó says. 'I don't know why they show those reels before children's pictures. It's one thing reading about a bombing in the newspapers but another seeing it on the big screen like that. Awful business.'

This reminds me of Sibby's question earlier. 'Mamó, Sibby was asking why Mr de Valera sent the fire engines when we're supposed to be neutral.'

'We are neutral, all right,' Mamó says, 'but most people are on the side of the Allies these days, and that includes Mr de Valera and the government. I think the Belfast bombing turned a lot more people in the south of Ireland against the Germans, to be honest. Sure, aren't we all on the same island after all? That's what Mr de Valera himself said when he was asked about the fire engines. And some people are even helping the Allies a wee bit, any way they can.'

'War, blooming war!' Sibby says. 'How much longer will it go on, Mamó? It's been two years now. Two whole years!' She groans and throws her hands in the air. 'I'm sick of the stupid war. It's all the grown-ups talk about.'

'Not too much longer,' Mamó says. 'You all right now, Grace?'

Mamó's kind eyes meet mine in the rear-view mirror. I nod and then look away.

'Try not to be worrying about the war, girls,' Mamó says. 'We're safe. Most of the fighting is far away in Europe and Russia. Sure nothing ever happens in Blacksod.'

'True,' says Sibby. 'Which is why I'll be leaving for Hollywood the minute I turn eighteen.'

Mamó laughs. 'Will you now?'

'I will,' Sibby says firmly. Then she looks at me and grins.

'Like Maureen O'Hara,' we both say together. It sets us off laughing so hard that Mamó can't help but laugh too. Sibby always makes me feel better when I'm worrying about things. She can be *a lot*, but I love her all the same.

* * *

Mamó insists on dropping me the whole way home. As she pulls up beside the lighthouse, she opens her driver's door.

'I can see myself in, Mamó,' I say, jumping out and closing the car door behind me. 'Thanks for a wonderful afternoon.'

'It was a pleasure, my love,' she says. 'It's not every day you turn ten. I want to have a quick word with Flora, but you run on ahead.'

'Thanks for the best present ever, Sibby!' I call through the open car window.

'See you tomorrow, kindred spirit,' she calls back.

I give her a big grin. 'See you!'

Flora must have heard the car's engine as she comes out to meet us in her green work overalls, which are streaked with fresh oil stains. Her bobbed red hair is tied back with a scarf, and there's a smudge of oil on her cheek too.

I've always called her Flora, ever since I was a baby. Not Mum or Mam. Everyone at school thinks it's strange.

'How was *Dumbo*?' she asks me, her Scottish accent making the elephant's name sound longer, *Duuum-booow*.

'The best picture ever,' I say.

'Flora, can I have a quick word?' Mamó says.

'Of course.' Flora smiles at me. 'You run on inside, pet. I'll join you in a second.'

As I walk towards the kitchen door, I can hear Mamó say the words 'newsreel' and 'bombing'. Darn it, I was hoping to forget all about that stupid newsreel, but no such luck.

We live in Blacksod Lighthouse. It's not the kind of building most people think of when you say 'lighthouse'; tall and white with red stripes banding it. Blacksod Lighthouse is square and pale granite grey, apart from the lantern, which *is* white, and the green wooden shutters over the windows. It's not that tall either. The lantern is at the top of a three-storey square tower, but it's plenty tall enough to safely guide ships into the bay, which is what it was built for. I know what year it was built too, 1864, as my dad is really into history.

There are six of us in the family if you include the dogs, which I do, of course. There's me, my seven-year-old brother Dannie, Flora, Dad, Poppy (or 'Poopy' as Dannie sometimes calls her as she's a bit daft and when she was a puppy she used to poo in the oddest places, like Dad's slippers) and Lucky (who's older and far more sensible).

When I walk inside, Dad and Dannie are sitting at the kitchen table and the dogs are under it. The table is covered in a sky-blue linen tablecloth and in the middle, on a china cake stand, is a Victoria sponge cake, with cream and strawberries squishing out the sides. My favourite! There are twisty little blue and white birthday candles stuck through the icing sugar on the top of the cake – ten, I'm guessing.

I grin. What a treat! I can't remember the last time we had an actual cake. There are food shortages on account of the war and lots of things aren't available.

I opened my birthday presents already, this morning at breakfast. I got a new book from Flora and Dad called *Swallows and Amazons*, and a big magnifying glass from Dannie and the dogs. I told Dad I wanted one for looking at insects, but I secretly want to see if I can use it to start a fire.

'Surprise!' Dannie jumps up from the table, making the dogs bark. 'Can we eat the cake now, Dad? I've been sitting here for ages and not putting my fingers in the cream, like you said.'

Dad smiles. 'You have. And once your mum's joined us, yes, you can have some cake. But Grace gets the first slice as she's the birthday girl.'

Flora walks in the kitchen door. 'Here she is now. Everything all right with Mamó?' Dad asks her.

She nods and smiles. 'All good.' She reaches into the top right-hand pocket of her overalls, pulls out a box of Friendly matches and carefully lights the candles.

'Blow them out and make a wish, pet,' she tells me. 'Quick, mind. I'm dying for a slice.'

I manage to blow out all the candles in one go, and I wish for the stupid war to be over. I know my little wish isn't going to make any difference, but it seems wrong to wish for stuff for myself when people's houses are being bombed.

'Did you bake the cake, Flora?' I ask, helping her pull the candles out. They make little clinks as we drop them onto a saucer.

She laughs. 'Ach, no, pet. Ellen made it this afternoon, bless her, while I was servicing the car.' Ellen is Sibby's big sister. The

Lavelles live just down the road, and Ellen is kind of like my big sister too. Me and Sibby have been best friends since we were tiny tots.

'That's why it looks so good,' Dad jokes.

Flora grabs a tea towel from the metal bar in front of the Waterford Stanley stove and swats him with it. 'You mind your manners, Tom Devine. I may be no cook, but I do have other talents. Like slicing cake.'

She takes a large knife out of the drawer and starts carefully dividing the cake into half, then quarters, then eighths.

Flora's right, she has a LOT of talents. My dad is the official Blacksod lighthouse keeper, but it's Flora who really runs the lighthouse and the weather station. And she looks after our old Ford car. And anything else that breaks around the house. Dad runs the post office and corner shop and spends a lot of his time there. It suits them both perfectly. He's very chatty and outgoing. Flora can be chatty too, when she wants to be, but she also likes time on her own to think. Spending all day pretending to be nice to people would exhaust her, she says.

The cake is delicious, the sponge light and fluffy, but my favourite bit is the cream and strawberries. Yum! We all tuck in.

'That Ellen can bake,' Dad says, sitting back in his chair and licking icing sugar off his fingers. He's polished off two slices.

Flora stands over him, tea towel at the ready. 'If you add that she'll make some lucky boy a fine wife one day, you know I'll swat you again, Tom.'

He grins. 'I know. Which is why I'd never say such a thing in this house, Flora.'

'Good!' Flora looks at me. 'So, tell us all about your trip to the picture house, Grace. What was *Dumbo* about?'

'A little elephant with big ears,' I say. 'He's in the circus and they make him dress up like a clown and do dangerous stunts. And then there's a very sad bit …' I tell them the story but not the ending, as I don't want to spoil it for Dannie. He might like to watch it some day.

When I finish, Flora says, 'Speaking of sad bits, Mamó said they showed a newsreel about the Belfast bombings before the picture. She said it upset you.'

I nod. 'It did a bit.'

'Do you want to talk about it?'

'Not really,' I say. 'But I still don't understand why the Nazis are bombing Ireland when we're supposed to be neutral.'

'In the south of Ireland, we are,' Dad says. 'But not in the north. They have a different government up there. They're part of the United Kingdom, remember? And they have a lot of factories in Belfast, and shipyards. That's what the Nazis were supposed to be bombing, not houses.' He calls them something rude under his breath.

'Mamó said that most Irish people are on the side of the Allies now. And that some people are even helping them a bit. Is that true?' I ask him. Dad looks at Flora and they lock eyes for a second. Am I imagining it or does she give him a tiny frown and a shake of her head?

Dad looks back at me. 'Maybe we can talk about this some other time,' he says. 'It's supposed to be your birthday tea. It's all getting a bit serious. And you know your mum doesn't like war talk.'

'You're right,' Flora says. 'I like peace talk. And the sooner this darned war is over, the better. For everyone.'

'Is Alfie still in the war?' Dannie says.

I look over at Flora, who sits up straighter in her chair and swallows. Alfie is her younger brother, our uncle. He lives in Edinburgh, where Flora is from, and he joined the British Army only a few months ago, just after his eighteenth birthday.

Before the war, he used to stay with us for a few weeks every summer. He took me and Dannie on adventures in our wooden fishing boat looking for sea monsters and made us laugh by dressing Lucky and Poppy up in human clothes. We wrote and put on daft plays together based on books he liked, like *Peter Pan* and *Treasure Island*, and we acted them out for Dad and Flora. Alfie said he'd like to be on the stage one day. Or be a teacher. He'd make a brilliant teacher, he's great fun.

'Yes, he's still in the war,' Flora says after a long pause. 'But he's not a solider, he's a medic, remember. He helps soldiers who are sick or wounded.'

'So he doesn't have a gun?' Dannie asks.

'No,' Flora says. 'Alfie's a Quaker, like me. We're pacifists, which means we don't like war and believe countries should talk to each other, not fight. That's why you learn German and French, so you can talk to people in different parts of the world in their own language.'

Dannie gives a little groan. I smile to myself. I find our German and French lessons with Flora easy – fun, even. We've been doing them for as long as I can remember. Flora says I have a knack for languages, but Dannie finds them difficult.

'Where is Alfie now?' Dannie asks.

'France, God love him,' Flora says. 'Don't ask me exactly where,

I don't know. He's not allowed to say.'

'Can we *please* talk about something else?' Dad says again.

'Yes, let's,' Flora says. 'And speaking of Alfie, that reminds me, he had a present sent over for you, from Edinburgh, bless him. It arrived weeks ago, and I'd forgotten all about it until now. Back in a second.' She leaves the kitchen for a moment and comes back in with a brown paper package, the size of a small shoebox. She hands it to me.

Dannie's eyes are out on stalks. Even though Dad runs the post office, we hardly ever get packages in the post, other than parts for the car or the weather instruments that Flora orders from Dublin.

I shake it, trying to guess what's inside. Flora hands me a pair of scissors. 'Careful now, I can reuse that string and paper.'

Once I get through all the packaging, I pause for a moment. 'Do you want to open the box, Dannie?' He loves opening things.

His eyes widen. 'Can I? Ace!'

I hand it to him. He pulls off the lid and lifts out something that is covered in layers and layers of old newspaper and nestled in even more newspaper, like an egg in a nest, keeping it safe. He passes it to me.

It's small but heavier than I expected. It must be something metal or stone. I unwrap it and stare down at my hands.

'Wow, Alfie's mini binoculars!' I say. Last time he was in Blacksod, he showed me how to use them to study the clouds. I turn them over in my hands. They are pretty special, and I can't wait to go outside and look through them.

'There's a card too,' Flora says, handing it to me.

It's in Granny's spidery handwriting. I pass it back to Flora to read. She's the only one who can make out the funny pen marks.

'Happy birthday to my favourite niece,' she reads. 'Think of me when you go cloud spotting in Blacksod. Wish I was there with you all. Much love always, Alfie XXX.'

'Good old Alfie,' Dad says. 'What a great present.'

'Can I go outside and test them out?' I ask.

''Course you can, love,' he says.

I look at Flora. She's gone quiet and still, which is unusual – she's never quiet or still. Maybe she's thinking about Alfie and France and the war.

She snaps out of it and gives me a smile. 'Happy birthday, Grace. I can't believe you're ten already. Where does the time go?' She gets up and gives me a big hug. She smells sweet, a bit like burnt toast. It must be the engine oil on her overalls. She breaks away and rubs my head. 'Now go outside and enjoy yourself. Tell those clouds I said hello.'

Cumulus

Known as fair-weather clouds,
they can look like balls of cotton wool

CHAPTER 1

THREE YEARS LATER

Sunday 7th May, 1944

'Look! There's a baby elephant, trunk and all. Like Dumbo!' I point up at the fluffy cumulus cloud drifting high above the Blacksod peninsula.

Flora smiles. 'You're right, it looks just like an elephant.'

It's a sunny Sunday afternoon and I'm lying on my back, cloud watching with Flora. I'm wearing shorts, and the scruffy marram grass that grows in the garden beside our lighthouse is tickling the back of my legs.

The cloud reminds me of my tenth birthday, when I went to see *Dumbo* with Sibby and Mamó. I can't believe I'm nearly thirteen – just over a month to go. A teenager! Sibby says you feel much older once you become a teenager, more like a real grown-up. She thinks she's an expert on teenagers as she's been studying her sister Ellen for years now. When Sibby started going on about spots and greasy hair and smelly armpits, it didn't sound like much fun, so I stopped listening to her. I wonder if she's right? Will I feel more grown up in a few weeks' time?

I spot something cutting through my cloud elephant, something long and black, its drone getting louder and louder like a giant angry beetle. An aeroplane! Another entry for my plane spotter's manual.

In the last three years, I've become a bit obsessed with plane spotting. When German planes fly over it makes me nervous, very nervous, but I still want to watch them and log them. And I like getting as many details down as possible. I know lots of the different types of planes now, from both sides of the war – Spitfires and Boeings and Heinkels.

Flora jumps up and brushes down the seat of her navy overalls. 'Better get inside, in case it's German.'

'But I need to get a better look. Can't we stay out one more minute? Please?'

'All right,' Flora says. 'But be quick, mind.'

I take my binoculars out of my pocket and press them to my eyes. 'Hello, Alfie,' I whisper to myself, like I always do when I use them.

As I watch, the details of the plane come into view, the heavy body with wheel bumps on its undercarriage, the black and white open cross shape on the underside of the wings, the swastika on the tail. It's German, all right. My stomach clenches, but I can't drag my eyes away yet. Not until I've seen as many details as I can.

This plane has extra glass panels over the cockpit, and it's chubbier than a fighter. It's flying so low I can almost make out the face of the pilot. And then I spot the weathervane symbol on its nose.

'It's a weather plane, not a bomber,' I say, my eyes watering a bit from squinting into the sun. 'A Junkers. A Ju 88, I think.'

'*Yun-kah.* You don't pronounce the J in German, remember? *Das Flugzeug ist ein Junkers.*'

I shush her. 'Flora! You can't speak German outside. You know Dad hates it.' I put on Dad's deep voice. '"Tut, tut, Flora. 'Tis the language of the enemy".'

Flora gives a laugh. 'He does, all right.'

The Junkers' roar is getting louder and louder. 'Weather plane or no weather plane, they'll still be armed,' Flora adds. 'Better not risk it. Come on inside now, pet.' She takes my arm and hoiks me to my feet.

Typical! I was having a lovely time lying here with Flora all to myself. It doesn't happen very often – she's always so busy these days. But I know she's right. We're safer inside the thick walls of the lighthouse.

'Stupid Germans,' I say huffily, stuffing the binoculars back into my pocket and then kicking at a tuft of grass. 'I'm sick of them. I hope they bloomin' well crash.'

* * *

Inside, Dad is sitting at the kitchen table, reading *The Mayo News*. He looks up. 'Has it started raining?'

'Nope, low-flying German plane,' Flora says. 'Weather plane, Grace thinks.'

'There was a weathervane on its nose,' I say.

'What's it doing in Mayo?' Dad asks.

'It's either lost or it's collecting weather data,' Flora says.

'It can't be lost,' I say. 'What about the Éire sign up on the hill? It must know it's Ireland.'

Last year lots of people, including Flora and me, helped to

spell out a huge ÉIRE in white stones on the hillside overlooking Blacksod Bay. These signs are supposed to show pilots that they're flying over neutral Ireland and not to drop bombs on us. There are stone numbers beside the signs too – Blacksod's number is 60 – and some people say these have only been given to the American and British pilots so they can navigate properly, not to the Nazis. I wonder if it's true.

'That sign is hard to miss, all right,' Flora says. 'They're probably just looking for weather information – air pressure, wind speed, the usual. As I'm always saying, they are not interested in bombing Mayo. It's nothing to worry about.'

I know she's saying this for my benefit, because I overthink things sometimes, and now and then I have nightmares of our village being bombed.

The mention of weather reminds me of something strange I overheard when I was having my breakfast. Flora and Dad were standing outside her office, but the door to the kitchen was open so I could hear them.

'Flora, who do you send your weather reports to?' I ask her now. 'Has it changed? I heard you talking to Dad earlier about the terrible crackle on the line. I remember because Dad joked it might be the Germans tapping the line, and you said not to joke about it, that it wasn't funny, that the clever folk at Dunstable had it covered. I thought the reports went to Dublin. Where's Dunstable?'

When I say the word 'Dunstable', Dad freezes, his newspaper stiff in his hands. Flora blinks a few times, and her ears go bright red.

'Of course we send them to Dublin,' she says. 'To the Met

Office, as usual. You must have heard me wrong. Now I must go and fix the toilet cistern.' She walks out of the kitchen quickly.

Dad puts down the newspaper and stands up. 'Have to help your mother in the office,' he says, which is nonsense as she just said she was off to fix the toilet. It's all very odd!

The office he's talking about is the office of the weather station. This is where Flora collects all the weather data and where many of the weather instruments are kept. There's the barometer in its big glass case. There's an instrument showing wind direction, which is wired to the wind vane outside, and a different instrument showing wind speed, which is wired to the anemometer, also outside. The anemometer is a long pole with four metal cups attached at the top that rotate as the wind blows. It drives Flora mad as it's always acting up! There are loads more weather instruments outside too, like the rain gauge and the thermometers in their Stevenson screen – a white wooden box covered in slats that stops the readings being affected by the sun.

Sometimes I help Flora read the different instruments and gather the information to write into the weather report book (she calls it the 'weather ledger'), which has columns for all the different readings, like wind direction and temperature.

Normally Dad has no interest in Flora's work. Something's going on, I know it. Something to do with the weather reports and somewhere called Dunstable. I know I heard it right as it's such a funny word – it rhymes with *constable*, like an English police officer – and I wanted to remember it, so I repeated it over and over in my head.

But what *is* happening? They've both been acting a bit strangely for weeks now. There have been a lot more phone calls to the office than usual, and Dad and Flora stop conversations as soon as I walk into the kitchen. It's all very suspicious. Which makes me want to know what's going on even more!

I go into my room and pull out my school atlas. It has maps of Ireland, Europe and the world. I study the map of Ireland carefully to see if I can find somewhere called Dunstable, but it's like looking for a needle in a haystack.

'Dunstable, Dunstable,' I say to myself. 'Where are you?' The word doesn't sound very Irish, and it's nowhere near Blacksod anyway. Next, I look at the area around Dublin – again, nothing. This is hopeless. Then I remember the super-duper atlas in Sibby's dad's study that has an index in the back. We used it for a geography project last year. I might find it in that.

'Just going to Sibby's,' I yell as I run down the hallway, through the kitchen and out the kitchen door, not stopping for an answer.

* * *

I let myself in the Lavelles' kitchen door. Mamó is stirring something on the stove. From the delicious meaty smell, it's some sort of stew.

'Hello, Mamó,' I say.

She nods at me and smiles. 'Always good to see you, my love.'

Ellen is sitting at the table, stabbing an orange with a needle attached to a medical syringe.

'Ellen, what are you doing to that poor orange?' I ask her.

'Practising injections,' she says, without looking up. 'The more practice I can get before I apply for medical school, the better.'

'Can girls go to medical school?' I ask, surprised.

Ellen puts the syringe down on the table and smiles at me. 'Grace! Of course they can. Girls can do anything they want. Sure isn't your mother a lighthouse keeper? The world is changing. And I want to be a doctor, even though everyone keeps telling me that nursing is better for girls. Like Dad and Mamó.' She looks over at Mamó.

'We just think it would be an easier road, chicken,' Mamó says. 'That's all.'

'I know nursing would be easier to get into than medical school, but I still want to try,' Ellen says. 'They're different jobs. Nurses are brilliant, but I have my heart set on surgery, not nursing. Sorry, Grace. You don't want to hear all this. Sibby's above in her room.'

'Thanks. And good luck with the injecting.'

I'm well used to the Lavelle family dramas by now! There's always something going on in their house. Mr Lavelle runs the fish factory in Belmullet and he works so hard he's barely at home. He even has a bed in the factory, Sibby says. Mrs Lavelle died years ago, when Sibby's little brother Liam was only a baby, so Mamó pretty much runs the house.

I run up the stairs and into Sibby's room. She's lying on her stomach, legs kicked up behind her, poring over one of her *Sunday Pictorial All-Star* annuals. She gets them every Christmas and they're full of photos of glamorous matinee stars.

'Sibby, I need to find somewhere called Dunstable in your dad's big atlas.'

She looks up from the annual. 'Why?'

I know I need to keep it to myself for the moment. Sibby loves secrets, but she's terrible at keeping them. I'll have to lie. Annoyingly I'm rubbish at making things up on the spot. I can't think of anything clever to say so I spit out, 'Alfie's there.'

'Your uncle, you mean?' she asks. 'The one in the British Army?'

'He's a medic, but yes. And please don't say anything to Flora about this. She doesn't like talking about the war. It upsets her.' That bit is true.

Sibby seems to have swallowed it. 'OK, let's go, Billy O.'

She shuts the annual and jumps off her bed. She runs down the stairs, into her dad's office, pulls the big atlas off the bookshelf and plonks it on the desk. She turns it over to find the index at the back. She's really quick and focused when she wants to be.

'Where are we looking for again?'

'Dunstable,' I say. 'D-u-n and then -stable, I think, like a horse's stable.'

'D,' she mutters to herself. 'D-u. Found it! Dunstable! It's in England. Page fifty-two. In box E4.' She turns to the right page, and running her finger over the paper, she locates it on the map. 'Quite near London.' Her eyes widen. 'Is he looking after injured soldiers in a hospital there? Heroes from the battlefields?'

'I guess so. Thanks, Sibby. See you tomorrow. And keep it to yourself, remember?'

She pretends to button her mouth shut. 'Mum's the word.'

As I walk home, my mind is spinning. And then it comes to me. Flora is giving weather reports to people somewhere near London. No wonder she and Dad have been acting strangely recently. Flora's helping the Allies!

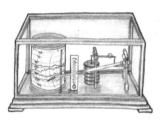

Stratus

Grey clouds that form a low layer over the ground

CHAPTER 2

Monday 8th May, 1944

On Monday morning, Sibby and I walk to school together as usual. It's grey out, but at least it's not raining. We walk up the road side by side, with Dannie and Sibby's younger brother Liam kicking stones along in front of us.

As we walk past the laneway to O'Shea's farm, Michael O'Shea jumps down off the stone wall and runs towards us. Was he waiting for us? *Strange.*

"Morning, Sibby,' he says, falling into step beside her.

I cough. 'Am I invisible?'

'Sorry, Grace,' he says with a grin. "Morning to you too.'

I'm expecting him to run on and catch up with the older boys who are along the road a bit, but he doesn't. He stays beside us. *Stranger and stranger.*

I look at Sibby, raising my eyebrows a little. She gives me a shrug.

'How are the puppies?' Sibby asks him. Michael's farm dog, Mabel, had puppies last week.

He smiles. 'I'm not supposed to say this, but they are as cute as buttons. Da says we can only keep one but I'm working on him to keep the lot, all seven of them.'

Sibby laughs. 'Good luck with that.'

'Thanks.' He walks with us for a few more minutes, chatting away easily about the puppies.

'Well, goodbye then, Sibby,' he says, giving her a little bow. 'And to you, Grace. See you in school.' And with that he runs on ahead, catching up with his friends.

'That was weird,' I say. 'He's never walked with us before.'

Sibby has a little smile on her lips.

'What?' I ask.

'I think he's madly in love with me,' she says, tossing her hair back. 'Don't blame him, I look ravishing today.'

'Utterly ravishing,' I say. 'And I know you're joking, but maybe he does like you.'

'You think?' She stops and stares at me. 'Are you being serious, Grace Devine?'

'I am, Sibby Lavelle. Deadly serious.' I look at her carefully. 'What do you think of him? Do you think he's handsome?'

'Sure I've known him all my life.' She looks up the road at Michael, who is currently doing a funny sideways walk, like a crab, showing off to the other boys. 'He's just Michael. He is quite funny though.'

He catches her looking at him and gives an enthusiastic wave, which Sibby returns.

'Yep,' I say. 'I'm pretty sure he likes you. Do you like him back?'

'What kind of question is that?' She sticks her head up in the air and starts walking faster.

'You do, don't you? You should tell him.'

'Are you crazy? Why would I do that?'

'You know.' I kiss the back of my hand, making smooching noises.

'Grace! Stop!' She looks around. 'Someone might see.'

I laugh. Her cheeks are going pink, which is unlike Sibby. She's not normally a blusher. 'You like him and you want to kiss him,' I say. 'Sibby and Michael up a tree, K-I-S-S-I-N-G.'

She shoves me with her shoulder. 'Stop! I do not. But I can't help it if I have an admirer. If I'm to be a matinee star, I'll have to get used to it.'

I laugh. 'You'll have boys all over Ireland swooning over you.'

'I will, and you'll be green with envy.'

I catch her looking at Michael again and I smile to myself. She really *does* like him.

* * *

At big break I'm playing football on the field with the boys when Michael runs up to me. It's his turn to help our teacher, Miss Waldron, to clean the blackboard between classes, so I'm surprised to see him.

'Grace, can I ask you something?' he says.

I'm goalie today and I'm crouched over low, watching the ball carefully. 'Yes, but quick while Mattie Reilly has the ball.'

'Would Sibby like a present, do you think?'

I look at him. 'What kind of present?'

He smiles. 'A nice one. We have puppies …'

I hear someone call my name. 'Watch out, Grace!'

I look back at the field. Mattie has lost the ball and Con is dribbling it up the grass towards me.

'Well?' Michael says. 'Will I call in to her after school, do you think? With one of the puppies. Would she like that?'

Con is now dangerously close to my goal. 'Yes, yes,' I say to Michael, not really listening to him. 'Now stop distracting me.'

I focus on the ball. Con swings his leg and boots it towards me. My reactions kick in and I throw my body sideways, my arms stretching out, out, out! I catch the ball and then fall towards the grass, holding it tight. Oof! I land on my shoulder and it hurts a bit.

There's a big cheer from the boys on my side.

'Nice save, Grace!' Mattie yells.

I pick myself up, throw the ball back into play and brush mud off the arm of my jumper. However I fell, I managed to rip it. Yikes, Flora's not going to be happy. And I'm going to have a big bruise on my shoulder too. But it'll be worth it if we win!

* * *

After school I'm sitting at the kitchen table finishing my homework, which is an English essay about my favourite season (summer, of course – school holidays!), when Sibby bursts through the door. Poppy and Lucky bark, then they realise it's only her and go back to their beds.

'I can't believe you told Michael to give me a puppy.' She throws her hands in the air. 'What were you thinking?'

'What are you talking about? I didn't tell him anything.' Then I remember the conversation at big break. 'Not exactly anyway. He asked me did you like presents and I said yes. Everyone likes presents.'

'Not from boys who might like them! It's embarrassing. Ellen and Mamó haven't stopped teasing me since they found it on the doorstep.'

I stare at her. 'He left a puppy on your doorstep?'

'Yes. In a cardboard box with my name on it. "To Sibby. With love, Michael."'

'Woohh! "With love." Did he draw lots of kisses on the box?'

'Stop! It's not funny.'

'Are you keeping the puppy?' I ask.

'No. Mamó says she has enough to be doing without a puppy peeing all over the place. It's only tiny. She marched straight up to O'Shea's with the box in her arms and handed it back. Poor little mutt must have been scared. He kept trying to eat the red bow around his neck.'

'Michael put a red bow on the puppy?' I'm pressing my lips together, trying not to laugh.

'It's not funny, Grace. None of this is funny. And I can't believe you encouraged him.'

'I was in the middle of a match,' I say. 'I was just trying to get rid of him. And he didn't say anything about giving you a puppy. He just said "present".' I stop for a second, trying to remember. Oops! 'Actually, he may have mentioned puppies.'

'Grace! I'm mortified and it's all your fault. Michael's going to think I'm a right eejit. Asking for a puppy and then sending it back.'

'You hardly asked for one. And I'm sorry. I was a bit busy trying to save a goal at the time.'

'You're not even supposed to be playing football with the boys.' She's right. Mattie's mother had already complained to Miss Waldron that it wasn't 'ladylike' and that I'd hurt myself, which is funny as I'm taller than her Mattie by a whole six inches. I still play and Miss Waldron pretends not to see me.

'I like playing,' I say. 'It's much better than sitting under the tree talking about boys.'

'We don't talk about boys,' Sibby says huffily. 'Not all the time anyway. And don't say anything to Michael about me ever again. Got it?'

'Understood. Now can I go back to my homework, please?'

'Fine! But you haven't apologised properly, Grace. And I really don't think you're taking my feelings seriously enough.'

'That's because you have a lot of them, Sibby. Too many for one person.'

'I'm sorry you feel that way.' She flounces out the door.

I think about going after her but I'm not sure I have the energy for it, so I sit back in my chair and give a big sigh. Sibby can be really annoying sometimes, but I shouldn't have said that about her having too many feelings.

Poppy raises her head and wanders over to me. I reach down and give her a rub under her chin. Dogs are far less complicated than people.

Stratocumulus

Low-level layers or patches of cloud that often
block out the sun

CHAPTER 3

Tuesday 9th May, 1944

On Tuesday when I call to Sibby's house to walk to school with her, Ellen answers the door.

'Sibby's gone on ahead,' she says. 'Sorry about that. Have you two had some sort of argument?'

'Kind of,' I say. 'But I was hoping she'd have forgotten about it by today.'

'Sibby?' Ellen raises her eyebrows at me. 'She can hold a grudge for weeks, you know that.'

My face must have dropped because she adds, 'I'm sure it'll be grand. Just give her a bit of time. And bribe her with biscuits. Works for me.'

I smile. 'Thanks, Ellen.'

But Sibby barely talks to me all day at school. I take Ellen's advice and give her some space. We've had arguments before and it's not nice, but it's always blown over in a few days. I'll write her a note and say sorry for the puppy business and for hurting her feelings. That should work.

* * *

When I get home from school and walk through the kitchen door, Dannie just behind me, the house is ghostly quiet.

'Flora?' I call. She's usually there waiting for us with a plate of shiny pink wafer biscuits or some other shop treat, taking a break from her work. We're so lucky Dad has a shop. If there are treats to be found in Mayo, he'll find them for his customers and for us, war or no war!

Flora likes to hear every little detail about school and what we've learned, especially anything sciencey. She used to be an engineer. She was in charge of a small factory in Scotland that made parts for cars, before she went to Dublin to do more study and met Dad. I think she misses having engineers to grill.

Flora's in charge of all the instruments at the lighthouse and the weather station, but if anyone asks what she does exactly – and sometimes they do, like when she's up a ladder checking the anemometer, which is forever getting stuck – we have to say that she is Dad's 'assistant'. Only people like the Lavelles and my teacher Miss Waldron, who is a friend of Flora's from the old days, know the truth.

'You'd think we were in the Dark Ages, not the 1940s,' Flora explained to me once when I asked her why we had to keep her real role a secret. 'People in Ireland can be funny about women working, especially when it comes to things like science and engineering. They don't think we're capable.'

'But that makes no sense,' I'd said. 'I'm just as good at science as the boys in my class.'

'I know you are,' Flora said. 'You keep studying and you'll get all the way to college and then the sky's your limit. I'll make sure of it, pet.'

I keep looking around the lighthouse for Flora. The dogs are missing too. They usually run out the kitchen door to meet us, all yapping and tails whipping around like windmills, excited to see us. Especially Dannie. They love Dannie. I tell him it's because he smells and they love stinky things! Maybe Flora left the garden gate open and they wandered off. But that's not like her to forget. Today – with no biscuits, no chat, no dogs, no Flora – something's different.

Then I spot her at the very far end of the garden, near the anemometer pole and the Stevenson screen. I must have walked straight past her. She's sitting rigidly on a kitchen chair with her legs stretched out in front of her and her arms folded across her chest, staring at the wall. Behind the wall is Blacksod Bay. That would be a normal thing to stare at – the sea, not a granite wall.

Something's wrong. Flora never sits still. She's always striding about the place, screwdriver or hammer in hand, humming away to herself. And why is she staring at a blank wall?

'I'll help you with your homework in a few minutes, OK?' I tell Dannie. 'I'm just going outside.'

'Homework?' He groans. 'Do I have to? Can't I play with the dogs first?'

I have no idea where the dogs are, so I make something up. 'They're out walking with Dad. You can play with them after.'

'Fine.' He flops down at the table and starts pulling his schoolbooks out of his satchel.

I walk out the kitchen door. 'Flora?' I say, making my way towards her. She doesn't turn her head to greet me. As I get closer, I see that she's gripping a piece of paper tightly in her hand.

'Flora,' I say again, a bit louder. She's still rigid. She doesn't budge or even blink.

I stand beside her, wondering what to do. Should I ring Dad at the post office? Where *are* the dogs? Poppy's rubbish on the road – she loves chasing cars and once she almost got knocked down. I'm starting to get really worried.

Flora looks down at the paper in her hand. It's a letter, written in Granny's spidery handwriting. She gives a deep sigh.

'Flora, what's wrong?' I ask. 'Please talk to me.'

She blinks a few times. 'Sorry, pet,' she says, snapping out of her trance. 'I was miles away. It's bad news, I'm afraid. Poor old Alfie. He didn't stand a chance. The entire medical tent was wiped out by a German bomb. No survivors.'

What? Did I hear her right? Alfie's dead? I feel hot all over and I hear a rush of blood in my ears. I bite my gum and take some deep breaths, trying not to cry. It's no use. There are tears in my eyes, and I wipe them away with the heels of my hands. I can't believe it! Not Alfie!

'I'm so sorry, Flora,' I manage, my voice small.

She nods. 'Me too. Alfie was the best.' Flora stops for a moment and swallows. 'He'll be buried in France with his army friends, and they'll have some sort of funeral service for them all. I hoped against hope that he'd survive the damned war, but it wasn't to be.' She gives a deep sigh. 'Hope is the thing with feathers, that perches in the soul.'

'And sings the tune without the words and never stops at all,' I finish. 'Emily Dickinson. We learned it at school.'

Flora gives a laugh. 'She's a good teacher, is Monica. I mean, Miss Waldron. You're lucky to have her.'

Above our heads, the anemometer rattles. Flora looks up at it and mutters something to herself about oil. Then finally she turns to look at me properly. Her eyes are red and glittering and a little wild looking. It frightens me, seeing her so upset.

'I'll miss Alfie,' I say. 'He was …' I can't think of anything else to say so I add, 'fun.'

She gives me the best smile she can. 'He was. Fun and kind. He had a big heart.'

There's a slapping noise from inside. I think Dannie's dropped one of his schoolbooks on the floor tiles. 'Could you fix your brother something to eat?' Flora asks. 'Tell him I'll be in soon. I just need a few minutes to myself.'

'Of course.' I go to hug her but she's in another world again, staring at the wall. I leave her alone.

As soon as I walk back into the kitchen, Dannie pounces. 'I'm starving. Are there any biscuits? Where's Flora?'

'She's outside. But don't go bothering her. She's thinking.' I'm not sure whether to tell Dannie about Alfie or leave it to Flora.

'What's happened?' he asks. 'You look all sneaky. Like you have a secret. And have you been crying?'

Maybe it will be easier for Flora if I tell him and get it over with.

'I have sad news,' I begin, realising as soon as the words are out of my mouth that I sound like a grown-up. I start again. 'Look, something really sad's after happening. It's Uncle Alfie, he was killed in a bombing in France.'

Dannie looks confused. 'I thought he was a doctor or something.'

'Medical officer. The tent he was working in was shelled. Flora's thinking about him outside.'

'Oh,' he says. 'That is really sad.' He goes quiet for a moment then adds, 'I'm going to draw Flora a picture of Alfie and the boat and the dogs and the lighthouse. To help her remember the good bits, when he was on holidays, not the war stuff. But can I have a biscuit first?'

I smile. Like Alfie, Dannie has a good heart. 'Let's see what we can find,' I say. I'll settle him down with a biscuit and some pencils and paper. Then I need to go and find the dogs.

* * *

That evening, dinner is quiet. Too quiet. Even Poppy's calm for once, lying under the table at Dannie's feet. Lucky's on his dog blanket in front of the stove. I found them halfway up Fallmore Road. Poppy was barking at a cow. I dragged her home by the collar.

Flora's usually full of questions for Dad, asking him for any news he's heard about the war from newspapers, or from people in the post office, or on the radio, which Dad has on all the time when he's at work, but right now she's not saying a thing. She's just sitting there, staring down at the half-eaten pork chop on her plate and rolling her peas around with her fork, like they're marbles.

'Anything interesting happen today, Dad?' I ask. 'Did Mrs Gillboy try to post her cat to Belfast again?' My voice sounds a bit too bright and chirpy, but I have to do something to fill the silence.

'There was something a bit different, in fact,' he says. 'And there's something we need to tell you ... about your mum's job. I took a phone call today from a lady in the Met Office. She couldn't get through to your mother.'

He looks at Flora, and Flora nods.

'Your mum needs to increase the weather reports,' he says. 'And she's going to need all our help. From six o'clock next Monday morning, they need to be done every hour.'

'Why?' I ask. 'Is it something to do with Dunstable?'

'It is,' he says. 'Flora, would you like to explain? It's time.'

Flora nods. 'It is. Since the war began, our weather reports have been sent to the Met Office in Dunstable, near London, through our own Met Office here in Ireland. But at the moment, we are dealing with Dunstable directly as it's quicker. The position of Blacksod is unique, you see. When the weather moves across from America and over the Atlantic Ocean, we are the first weather station in Europe to experience that particular weather system. Are you with me so far, both of you?'

I nod.

'Yes,' Dannie says. 'I think so. We get the weather from America and the ocean first. So we're important.'

'That's right. Very important.' Flora gives him a smile. 'So if a storm is coming that direction, from the west, we see the signs well before England or France. An increase in wind, a drop in barometer readings, that kind of thing. And as your dad says, from Monday next week we need to ring in weather reports every hour.'

'Even during the night?' I ask.

Flora nods. 'Until midnight, yes. Then every three hours until 6am. The 3am one will be the killer.'

'Why do they need a weather report at three in the morning?' I ask.

'It's a very good question. I've been thinking about it ever since your dad told me about the phone call.' Flora's voice is surprisingly animated for someone who's been so quiet for most of dinner. 'It sounds like the Allies are planning something. Something important that involves the weather over the Atlantic. Tom, did the lady say anything else about the weather reports? Anything at all?'

Dad shakes his head. 'Not that I can recall.' He thinks for a second. 'Oh, hang on, there was something else. She said not to go telling anyone about the extra reports. That the folks in Portsmouth wouldn't like it. That it's top secret. I remember thinking it was odd, since the Met Office is in Dunstable, not Portsmouth.'

'Aha!' Flora gives a short laugh. 'You know who she's really reporting to, don't you?'

Dad looks a little baffled.

'Come on, Tom!' she says. 'Portsmouth! Who's based in Portsmouth? Eisenhower and the Allied leaders, that's who! That's why it all has to be so hush-hush. Remember the man who was over a couple of years ago? James Stagg. The Scottish man. We had a quick meeting with him. I bet she works with him. You were talking to him too, weren't you, Grace?'

'Yes,' I say. 'He told me about his nieces in Glasgow and how much he missed them.' He was the first Scottish person I'd met in Blacksod, apart from Flora and Alfie of course, so I remember it well. We don't get too many visitors – it's not exactly the kind of place people go on their holidays, unless they are lighthouse nuts. I'd been at the harbour watching the seagulls hopping around, pecking at bits of fish guts, taking a break from my plane spotting when I bumped into him.

Dad smiles. 'Aye, I remember him all right. Tall, red-haired lad with a moustache. Said he'd like to come back one day to fish. Said he worked as a meteorologist for the British Army, a weather man.'

'That's him!' Flora says, getting more and more animated. 'He said we might hear from his office one day, and today was clearly that day. We need to take this seriously, Tom. Never miss one report. Make sure they are accurate. Lives may depend on it. The war even.'

'Flora!' Dad gives her a look and then side-nods at me and Dannie.

'What?' Flora says. 'Spit it out, Tom.'

Dad looks a bit awkward. His mouth twists around a bit and then he says, 'Maybe we should talk about this later.'

'Are you trying to say, not in front of the children?' Flora says. 'Is that it? Alfie was eighteen when he joined up, only five years older than Grace. Our children are clever and brave. We can trust them to keep an important secret. Grace, Dannie, look at me. If you tell anyone about the call from Dunstable or the weather reports, someone else's brother might be in danger, do you understand? They might even die.'

Dannie's eyes widen. He leans down to pet Poppy.

'Flora!' Dad says. 'You're scaring them.'

Her eyes flash. 'We're in the middle of a war, Tom. We should all be scared. Bloody scared. A horrible, pointless, stupid war. A war where real people get killed. Like my lovely Alfie. He didn't … I can't …' Her eyes start to well up with tears. She stands up abruptly, making the legs of her chair screech against the tiles. 'Excuse me.' She gives the door an almighty shove and strides through it, leaving it swinging behind her.

Dad gets up, closes the door, and then turns back towards me and Dannie. 'Your mum's upset about Alfie. She's not herself. She didn't mean to worry you.'

'They won't get us here, will they, Dad?' Dannie says, his eyes still wide. 'The Germans, I mean.'

'No, son. We're neutral, remember?'

'So are Switzerland and look what happened to –' I start to say.

Dad gives me one of his stern looks and I stop talking. Dannie's face is getting whiter and whiter, and I know I'm not helping. He can be sensitive sometimes.

'Dad's right, Dannie,' I say. 'The fighting's hundreds of miles away, in mainland Europe. The Germans aren't interested in Ireland. We're far too small for them to bother about.'

Dannie seems happy enough with this. 'OK. I still won't tell anyone about the weather stuff, just in case,' he says. 'Not even Liam. I'll keep it a top-secret kind of secret.'

Dad ruffles his hair. 'Good man. Now can you help Grace clear the dinner? I'll just go outside and check on your mum.'

* * *

That was all a bit dramatic, I think as I stand at the Belfast sink and pick up a dirty plate. Like something that would happen in Sibby's house! Flora's not usually so dramatic. She must be seriously upset.

I dip the plate in the sudsy water and scrub it clean with the dish brush, thinking about what Dad and Flora said about keeping it all a secret. As I pass the plate to Dannie to dry, it occurs to me that at least he has someone to keep a secret *from* – his best friend Liam. Since yesterday and my big falling out with Sibby, I have no-one to tell a secret *to*.

Altostratus

A mid-level grey, overcast layer of cloud which often
produces light drizzle

CHAPTER 4

Wednesday 10th May, 1944

On Wednesday after school, I have an important job to do. So important that my hand is shaking while holding the heavy black telephone receiver. Flora has trained me carefully, going over and over what I'm to say, but I'm still nervous. I swallow, take a deep breath, then dial the English number.

'Hello, this is Dunstable 2100,' a lady says, clear as a bell. 'How may I help you?'

I'm surprised by how good the line is *and* by the lady's voice. Flora said they moved the Met Office out of London on account of all the bombings. Dunstable is about thirty miles from London, but the lady doesn't sound like she's from Dunstable or London or anywhere else in England. It throws me for a moment. My hand shakes even more.

I've helped Flora take all the readings from the instruments and put them in the weather ledger before, but I've never rung in the weather report myself. But today is different – today it's my job and mine alone, as Dad and Flora need my help. Dad is working at the post office and Flora is up a ladder fixing the anemometer, which is on the blink yet again.

It took ages for Flora to talk Dad around. He thought I was too young to ring in the reports.

'Too female, more like,' I overheard Flora say. 'If Dannie was nearly thirteen, I bet you'd let him help. She's perfectly capable, Tom. More than capable.'

Dad protested but Flora managed to talk him around. So I can't let her down now!

Come on, you can do this, Grace, I tell myself. It's just a telephone call.

'Hello, is anyone there?' the voice asks again.

'Yes, sorry. This is Blacksod Weather Station in County Mayo. I'm ringing in the 2pm weather report.'

'The 14:00 hours report, you mean?'

'Yes, sorry, the 14:00 hours weather report.' Darn it, I'd forgotten to use the twenty-four-hour clock. I can hear the wobble in my voice, and I clutch the receiver even harder.

'Thank you, Blacksod in County Mayo, Éire. Go ahead, please.' And there it was – she said 'Mayo' and 'Éire' in a lilting uppey-downey way, not in a flat English way.

'Are you Irish?' I ask.

She laughs. 'I am indeed. Grew up in Bantry. I've lived here for years. But we'd better get back to the report, my supervisor's staring at me. The readouts, please?'

'Of course, sorry.

Barometer 23.8 falling slowly by -2

Wind speed direction WSW, west south west

Wind speed 5 knots

Temperature 50 degrees Fahrenheit

Visibility 8 …'

I continue with the weather report, giving detailed information on the cloud cover – the form, amount of cloud, and height of the base from the ground in hundreds of feet – with all the relevant figures. When I've finished, the Met Office lady says, 'Thank you …' She pauses for a moment and I hear a rustling noise, like a piece of paper being turned over. 'Mrs Devine, is it?'

'I'm Grace Devine, her daughter. Mrs Devine's fixing the anemometer.'

'Is she now? Good for her. Thank you, Grace. I'm Maureen and I'll talk to you again, I'm sure. Enjoy the rest of your day.'

'Thank you too, Maureen.' I put down the receiver, feeling proud of myself. My first solo weather report! I skip outside with a big smile on my face.

'Flora,' I call up the ladder. 'I did it. The lady on the phone from Dunstable was Irish. Isn't that gas? Maureen was her name.'

'Good for you,' Flora says, then climbs down the ladder, one of the cups from the anemometer in her hand. 'I'll have to drive into Belmullet and get some new fittings to fix this.' The anemometer rattles loudly above our heads. 'Darn it, I should have taken the whole thing down. It doesn't sound happy up there. I don't want more of the fittings to break. I swear that instrument is cursed!'

'I can take it down,' I say. 'I'll be careful, I promise. You go on to Belmullet.'

She looks at me for a moment, as if weighing this up.

'Look, I'm already wearing my overalls,' I say. I put them on before giving the weather report to give me confidence – old green ones of Flora's with the arms and legs rolled up a little.

She looks me up and down. 'So you are. I like the boots. Very practical.' They're an old brown lace-up pair of Flora's that fit me perfectly.

'I'm capable, Flora, you said so yourself,' I add.

'You heard me talking to your dad, did you?' She smiles. 'Ach, I'm in a hurry so you're on. All you need to do is to loosen the screws that hold the instrument to the pole and the whole anemometer should lift off. Be careful now, it's heavier than it looks.' She hands me her screwdriver and I put it in one of my pockets.

Overalls are excellent – they have massive pockets. Why don't skirts and dresses have decent pockets, ones big enough for important stuff like screwdrivers and binoculars? That's what I want to know! That's why I prefer overalls or shorts. Flora lets me wear them all the time, except for at school. It's skirts only for the girls at school. Although I always have a pair of shorts stashed in my bag for break time football.

'I want Dannie to hold the bottom of the ladder though,' Flora adds. 'Just in case.'

She walks towards the lighthouse. 'Dannie! Can you come out here, Dannie!' She calls loudly. All the windows are open so he should be able to hear her.

Once she spots him walking out the kitchen door, followed by the dogs, she gets going, jumping into our old black Ford and starting up the engine, which rumbles and bangs a bit before igniting. Petrol is pretty scarce these days on account of the war rationing, so she only drives when it's urgent.

'Back soon, you two,' Flora yells out the car window. She gives us a wave and speeds off, sending the gravel under the wheels flying and making the dogs bark. Flora likes to drive fast. Dad's always giving out to her about it.

I hear the roar of another engine, this time coming from the sky.

I look up, expecting to see an aeroplane – it certainly sounds like an aeroplane's engine – but I can't see anything. I squint up my eyes. I can see something ... a faint gap in the cloud layer where a plane has cut through it.

Dannie stomps towards me, the dogs at his heels. 'I was doing this ace drawing,' he tells me, 'of British soldiers shooting Germans on a beach in France. Pow, pow, pow!' He shoots me with his finger. He's been a bit war obsessed since he heard about Alfie yesterday. Dad wanted to stop him drawing violent pictures and make him draw something else instead, but Flora says it's his way of dealing with the news. So he's allowed draw as many war pictures as he likes, for the moment at least.

Flora's mood has been a bit unpredictable since the news about Alfie too. You wouldn't know what she'd say or do. One minute she's all quiet and the next minute she's a bit manic, chasing Poppy around the garden. Dad says it's grief, on account of Alfie. I'm sure he's right.

'Will you put your foot on the bottom rung of the ladder to stop it from slipping, please?' I ask Dannie. 'I'll pass you down the anemometer in a minute. I just need to unscrew it first.'

'How long will it take? I want to get back to my picture.'

'Not long.'

I climb up the ladder. When I reach the top, I'm about to take the screwdriver from my pocket when I hear another roar and then a loud bang, like something has exploded. I look right, over towards the hill where the noise came from. There's a pillar of smoke rising from one of the fields. Then I hear loud popping noises. *What on earth?*

The dogs are barking wildly, and Poppy is racing up and down the grass.

'Shush, you two,' I shout down at them. After a moment they go from barking to growling. Poppy's nose is up in the air. She must be able to smell something. She may be daft, but she's got the nose of a bloodhound and the hearing of a wolf.

'What was all that noise?' Dannie asks.

'I'm not sure.' I pull my binoculars quickly out of my pocket and automatically whisper 'Hello, Alfie' to myself. It gives me a bit of a start. I blow out my breath to calm myself. It's the first time I've said it since the news about Alfie and I have mixed feelings about it. Maybe I'll stop saying it, but I don't want to forget about him either.

Grace, concentrate! I tell myself. Think about it later. I put the binoculars to my eyes and focus on trying to find out where the smoke is coming from.

As I watch, plumes of toxic-looking black smoke fill the air. Is it a gorse fire? They do happen sometimes in the summer. But what about the noise?

I lower the binoculars down, down, towards the ground. And then I see it. I get such a fright that I wobble on the ladder and I have to put out a hand to steady myself.

Contrail

A long slash of white against the blue sky, made by an aircraft.
Short for condensation trail. When a plane cuts a gap though the cloud,
it's called a distrail

CHAPTER 5

Wednesday 10th May, 1944

'Grace!' Dannie calls up at me. 'What is it? What's happening?'

'There's an aeroplane. On Fallmore Hill. It's crashed and it's on fire.'

'A plane? What kind of plane? German? British?'

I look again, squinting my eyes to try and make out any symbols on the plane's body or wings, or even what type of plane it is. 'I can't see with all the smoke.'

I put the binoculars away and scramble down the ladder, too quickly – I miss a rung with my foot and bang my knee hard against the wood of the frame. Luckily, I was holding on tight. I pause for a second, take a deep breath, and then start climbing down again, slower this time. Everything feels heightened. My blood is thumping through my body and my head is racing.

Why is Flora not here? She'd know what to do. But she's on the way to Belmullet now and Dad's in the post office. He's a good twenty minutes away from Fallmore Hill even if he runs. We're much nearer, three or four minutes at a sprint.

It's up to me. I'm going to have to do something. I stand on the grass at the bottom of the ladder, my hands gripping the wood. I close my eyes. *Think*, Grace, *think*!

From what I could see, the fire hasn't reached the fuel tanks yet; it seems to be concentrated over one of the engines. There are pilots and airmen in that burning plane. If they're to have any chance of survival, we have to do something and quick!

'OK, here's what we need to do,' I tell Dannie. 'Ring Dad in the post office and tell him what's happened. He'll ring the fire station and the ambulance service.'

Dannie's face is pale, but he nods. 'What then?'

'I'm going to the hill.'

'I'm coming with you.'

'Are you sure? You don't have to.'

'I want to.'

'OK then. We have to be fast.' While Dannie runs inside to the office to ring Dad, the dogs following behind him, I find Flora's black leather first-aid bag in the cupboard in her office and grab the multi-coloured crochet blanket from the back of the armchair by the stove.

Dannie joins me in the kitchen. 'Did you talk to Dad?' I ask him.

'Yes. He's going to ring the services and then come up to the hill. He said he'll bang on some doors on the way and find a few more people to help.'

'That's a good idea. Let's try the Lavelles' house. We'll be going past it anyway!' I dash out the door. The heavy leather bag I'm clutching bangs against my calves as I run. Dannie is just behind me, the dogs too.

'Put the dogs back inside,' I tell him.

'They might be useful,' Dannie says.

'Useful? Those two? They'll be as useful as a chocolate teapot.' I stare at him. His eyes are wide and he looks scared. He's always better with the dogs around so, although I think he's gone

57

crackers, I say, 'Fine. But you're in charge of them. And put Poppy on her lead.'

* * *

I bang on the Lavelles' door, hard, so full of adrenaline I can feel it tingling in my fingers. 'Come on, answer,' I say. I bang again and again. Dannie stays at the gate with the dogs.

The door swings open. It's Sibby. She glares at me. 'What do *you* want? And what's with all the knocking?'

'Never mind all that,' I say in a rush. 'There's a plane on fire on Fallmore Hill. The airmen may still be alive. We need to help.'

She looks at me for a second and then takes in the bag and the blanket. 'You're serious?' she says.

'I'd hardly joke about dying airmen, Sibby.'

'I guess,' she says. 'Dad's not here. It's just me and Mamó and Liam. Oh, and Ellen, but she's washing her hair. She'll probably be too busy.'

'Grab them all and come on then!' I say.

Ellen appears in the hall with a towel wrapped around her head, Liam just behind her. 'What's going on?'

'There's a plane on fire on Fallmore Hill,' I explain. 'Dad's ringing the emergency services but I'm going up there to see if I can help.'

'Jeepers!' Ellen says. 'Why are we standing around talking then? Let's go!' She pulls the towel off her head and flings it on the ground.

'That's what I said,' I mutter under my breath.

'Mamó!' Ellen hollers down the hall. 'Grace, you go with Liam and Sibby and I'll catch up with you. I'll bring Mamó. She's pretty useful in an emergency. But don't go doing anything stupid, Sibby.'

'Why would I do anything stupid? What about Liam?' Sibby says.

'He's a sensible lad, he can take care of himself,' Ellen says. 'You, on the other hand …'

Sibby's eyes flash. 'That's so unfair. You're always –'

'Stop gabbing and come on!' I grab Sibby's arm and start pulling her down the path.

'This doesn't mean we're friends again,' she huffs as we run up Fallmore Road towards the side of the hill. 'You're too bossy, Grace Devine.'

'And you talk too much,' I say. 'Just run!'

There's another loud bang, like a car tyre blowing out, which sets the dogs off again. It must have come from the plane. Dannie jumps at the noise and drops Poppy's lead. Poppy starts running towards the noise but Liam darts after her and manages to grab her lead again. He hands it back to Dannie and gives him a squeeze on the shoulder. Liam's a bit older than Dannie and has always been kind like that.

Dannie nods and the boys and dogs start running even faster.

I speed up too, but the first-aid bag and blanket are slowing me down. I stop for a second and switch the bag into my other hand.

'Oh, give me that thing.' Sibby grabs the bag and holds it against her chest, like a baby. She takes the blanket and puts it on top of the bag. 'Go!' she says.

I sprint past everyone, towards the crash. I've always been a strong and fast runner, but today I have reason to run like the wind.

* * *

When I reach the gate into the field, I stop dead. I knew what I was going to see – a crashed plane – but what's in front of my eyes is really scary. The size of the aeroplane is overwhelming: a huge lump of metal, angry grey against the green and brown of the grass and heather, its left wing badly damaged by the crash landing. The air is thick with the sharp, nose-burning smell of smoke, and I can almost feel the roar and the heat of the flames even from here.

It's a German plane, a Junkers, like the one I'd seen soaring through the sky earlier in the week when I was in the garden with Flora. I feel bad now that I'd willed one to crash. What a horrible thing to think! I brush the thought away and concentrate on studying the plane. The body and the right wing are still intact, but the canopy over the cockpit and the entire tail are missing.

There's another ear-splitting bang, this time like a hundred car tyres blowing out at the same time, followed by another bang, then another. There's more smoke, then a tower of flame lights up the sky, accompanied by billowing smoke.

As I stare in horror, the others catch up with me.

'The left engine has just caught fire,' I shout over the noise.

There's a round of cracks so sharp I have to press my hands over my ears to stop it from deafening me. The dogs are barking wildly at the noise. Poppy is straining at her lead, but Dannie is holding firm.

'And there goes the ammunition in the heat,' I say. 'You all need to stay here. Whatever happens, do not go into the field.'

I try opening the gate, but it's tied shut. It would take me ages to untie the rope holding it closed so I start to climb over instead.

'Where do you think you're going?' Sibby says.

'To see if there are any survivors.'

'Germans, you mean?' Liam says. 'Nazis?'

'They're still people,' I say.

'Yeah, I suppose,' he says. He doesn't sound all that sure.

But I *am* sure. No-one deserves to be burned alive, even Nazis.

Sibby goes quiet for a second. Then she says, 'I'm coming with you. Liam, stay with Dannie and the dogs. Don't move, OK?'

Liam nods. 'Yeah, OK.'

'It's dangerous, Sibby,' I say. 'I'm not sure –'

'Now you're the one talking too much. We do this together or we don't do this at all. OK?'

I feel spikes of fear running up my spine. I'll be glad to have Sibby beside me, to be honest. I take a deep breath to try and steady my nerves. 'OK.'

'Boys, we need you to stay calm,' she says. 'If anything happens, go and get help. Whatever you see, do not go into the field. Understand?'

And she calls *me* bossy? Luckily I don't say this out loud.

The boys nod.

'Be careful,' Dannie says, his voice wobbling a bit.

'We will,' we say together.

I climb quickly over the gate. Sibby shoves the first-aid bag and the blanket into Liam's arms and climbs over after me.

Cap clouds

Clouds that form around mountain summits and look like hats
on the mountain's head

CHAPTER 6

Wednesday 10th May, 1944

'This way,' I tell Sibby over the roar of the flames, pointing to the front of the Junkers. The left wing is missing – it must have ripped off when it hit the hill. The wheels and undercarriage are buried in the boggy and stony soil on the side of Fallmore Hill, and the whole body of the plane is lurching to the left.

'Towards the cockpit,' I say. 'If the pilot's alive, that's where he'll be with his crew.'

It doesn't look good – the glazed canopy that should be shielding the cockpit and the airmen inside isn't there. It must have been ripped off too.

'How many men in total?' Sibby asks.

'Three, sometimes four. We should stay together. It's safer.'

She nods. 'You know planes. I'll follow you.'

That's a first, I think to myself. Sibby usually wants to lead. But I keep that to myself too.

'Stay low,' I say, 'in case there are any more ammo rounds to go off.'

We start running in a wide loop towards the front of the plane, bent so low we're almost sweeping the ground. It's not easy. We have to jump over rocks, and now and then my foot gets stuck in a boggy bit and I fall over. Luckily my boots are nice and solid; I could have been in my canvas plimsolls like Sibby. I just get straight back up again and wipe my muddy hands on the front of my overalls.

Before I have the chance to get near the cockpit, I hear barking beside me. It's blooming Poppy, jumping over the rocks like a crazed rabbit, dragging her lead behind her. I look over at Dannie and Liam. Liam starts to climb over the gate, but I gesture at him with both hands to stay put. I'll deal with it.

'Poppy! Go back, you stupid mutt.' I wave my hands at her, shooing her away.

But she won't stop barking. Then she sinks her teeth into the trouser leg of my overalls and starts pulling. I manage to shake her off.

'For goodness' sake, Poppy.' I reach down to grab at her lead, but she runs away, towards the very back of the cockpit. She stands there, barking frantically.

'What's she doing?' Sibby asks.

'I have no idea, stupid dog.'

Then I spot what she's barking at: a dark shadow. I squint my eyes, trying to make it out through the smoke. It's the head and arms of an airman. He's trying to climb out of the plane. He seems to be caught – the top of his body is over the edge of the cockpit, but he's stuck in some way.

I feel bad for yelling at Poppy now. She's not so stupid after all! I run towards Poppy and the man, Sibby just behind me. When we reach him, the heat is so intense it's like being in an oven and the hot, acidy smoke makes me cough.

He's still trying to get out, his hands pushing against the metal side of the plane. He must have spotted Poppy as he's saying '*braver Hund, braver Hund*' over and over again. That means 'good dog' in German. It gives me a start. I've never heard German spoken by an actual German person before, just Flora.

'*Ihr Name ist Poppy*,' I say loudly. Her name is Poppy.

He looks over at me in shock. It must be pretty odd seeing a dog and two girls in a field, one of whom speaks a bit of German. But he gets over it quickly. Far quicker than Sibby, who is staring at me like I'm an alien from outer space. She has no idea about Flora's German and French lessons. I've never told her. She thinks I'm a big enough swot as it is.

'*Du sprichst Deutsch?*' he asks. Do you speak German?

'*Ja.*' I try to think of the words for 'a little'. '*Ein bischen.*'

He gabbles something so quickly I can't make it all out. But I do understand the word *bein* – leg. And *sitzplatz* – seat. And *bein gefangen* – leg caught.

'I think his leg is trapped,' I tell Sibby. 'If it's the seatbelt I might be able to cut it away. I have a pocket-knife in my overalls.' I pat my top left-hand pocket.

'Course you do!' Sibby gives a short laugh. 'You speak German and you carry a weapon. Anything else you haven't told me?'

'I'll explain later. I'm going to see if I can free him.' I touch the metal of the cockpit. It's red hot. I take my work gloves out of my bottom right pocket and pull them over my hands. 'Give me a leg up so I can get inside.'

'Inside?' Sibby practically shrieks. 'Oh, no. That's a bad idea. A really bad idea. What if something happens to you?'

'I'll be fine. Put your hands like this.' I show her how to make a cradle for my foot with her hands.

'For the record, I still think this is a terrible idea,' she says.

'We can't just leave him there to burn.'

I hear her mutter something that sounds like 'stubborn ninny', but I ignore her.

The airman groans.

'*Halte durch*,' I tell him. Hang in there. '*Ich komme.*' I'm coming.

'Over here, Sibby.' I point at the side of the cockpit to the left of the man. If I'm right about the Junkers 88, there should be some floor space in front of the pilot's seat. I put my muddy work boot on her hands. She winces but holds my weight.

'Be careful,' Sibby says.

'I will.'

She takes my weight then lifts her hands, hooshing me upwards. I fall over the lip of the cockpit and into the Junkers, my hands and then body hitting the floor with a crunch. It's littered with glass. I'm glad of my gloves and my overalls. I look at the pilot and co-pilot seats. They're empty. For a moment I wonder where the other airmen are, but then I hear a groan from the man at the back of the cockpit, which makes me focus.

I look towards him. I can barely make him out. There's smoke everywhere. It's in my eyes and in my throat. I cough strongly, my body rejecting the fug.

Come on, Grace, I tell myself. *Get moving!* I inch myself forwards, crawling across the hot, hot floor. The man is just in front of me, his upper body resting on the lip of the cockpit. I was right! He's stuck. I rub my watering eyes so I can see and keep crawling until I'm in front of him.

One of his legs is trapped because there's a large piece of bone sticking out of the calf and the material of the seatbelt is caught in the splintered bone. Yuck, disgusting! My stomach lurches at the sight of it!

There's another loud bang from somewhere in front of me.

'Hurry up, Grace,' Sibby yells. Her head pokes over the edge of the cockpit for a second and then disappears and reappears again. She must be jumping up and down. 'There are more flames now.'

I try pulling at the seatbelt but it's not budging. I press the catch, hard. It won't give way.

I know what I have to do, so I concentrate. I take off my gloves, pull out my pocket-knife, and start hacking at the seatbelt just below the man's broken bone.

He groans.

'*Es tut mir Leid*,' I say. Sorry. But I keep going.

It's getting hotter and hotter in here and sweat is prickling my back. The smoke is engulfing us, making us both cough violently.

Every time the man coughs, he groans in pain. Poor thing!

Keep going, Grace, I tell myself. *Nearly there.* Finally, snap! The last strand of the seatbelt webbing gives way and he's free.

'*Gehst du*!' I yell at him. Go!

'Sibby, pull his arms!' I shout. I stand on the seat and shove him as best I can, upwards, over the lip of the cockpit.

He's almost out now. But then he slumps.

'Sibby, I think he's passed out! It's up to us now,' I shout. 'One last huge pull on three, OK?'

'OK,' she yells back.

Then I hear another voice. 'And we're here too, Grace. Me and Mamó.'

It's Ellen. I nearly cry with relief.

'One,' I say. 'Two. *Three!*'

I put both my hands on his hips and give an almighty push and finally, whoosh, he's out. It's just me in the cockpit now.

There's another ear-splitting cracking noise. This time as well as hearing flames I can see them, licking at the electronic instruments at the back of the cockpit. And the heat! It's ferocious! It's like being in the middle of a Hallowe'en bonfire.

'Get out of there, Grace!' Sibby yells. 'Right now! Get out! Out! Out!' She sounds in such a panic that it jolts me into action.

I scramble onto the seat and up over the lip of the cockpit. I see Mamó down below me, her arms outstretched.

'Jump, Grace,' she says. 'Into my arms.' Anyone else and I would have thought twice, but not Mamó. She's strong as an ox. So I jump.

With a *womph*, I hit her body. She stumbles backwards a bit and then stops. I'm in her arms, shocked but safe.

'You all right?' she asks, putting me down.

'I think so.'

'Good. Now run! The cockpit is about to blow!'

Crepuscular rays

Sunbeams that appear to be bursting from a
cumulus cloud

CHAPTER 7

Wednesday 10th May, 1944

Mamó and me run as fast as we can towards the gate, dodging the rocks. In front of us, through the plumes of smoke, I can see Sibby and Ellen supporting the airman between them, his broken leg dangling like a puppet's limb.

There's another almighty bang behind us. I turn my head. The whole Junkers is engulfed in flames, including the cockpit.

I feel a rush of emotion. I stop dead and instantly start crying, huge sobs so strong I can feel the shudder of them right through my body.

'You're all right, Grace,' Mamó says, rubbing my back firmly. 'It's just shock. You saved a life. That's quite something.'

When we make it to the gate, Sibby and Ellen have put the airman down on the ground. Ellen has rolled the blanket up and put it under his head to make him feel more comfortable.

'I sent Dannie and Liam off to knock on any doors they can find to get help,' Ellen says.

'Good thinking,' Mamó says.

The dogs seem to have gone with the boys. Probably just as well. Poppy would be trying to lick the airman's face right now otherwise.

'I have the first-aid bag here,' Ellen says.

'Let's see what we have to play with,' Mamó says, opening it up and looking inside. 'It seems pretty well stocked, thank goodness. Good woman, Flora. Morphine, thank God.'

As they rummage through the bag, I kneel beside the airman. I pull off my gloves. My hands are stinging. They're red with burns and littered with small cuts. Broken glass must have pressed through the leather of the gloves. But it's nothing compared to the man's injuries. He has vivid red and black burns on his cheeks and chin, and the skin on his hands is so black I have to look away. And his poor leg with the snapped bone. I can't bear to look at that either!

I kneel down beside him and focus on his face. He's young, he looks around Alfie's age. I try not to think about my uncle and how scared he must have been right before he died. All those bombs, all that noise, all that fire!

The German airman is in so much pain his eyes are screwed shut. His heavy grey trousers are scorched and ripped, and he reeks of smoke. The leather of his grey flight jacket is singed black in places. Better the jacket than his skin though. He's making a low groaning noise under his breath and his body is shaking. His eyes are still shut.

'*Es wird dir gut gehen*,' I tell him in German. You're going to be all right.

He opens his eyes and looks at me. They're a deep navy blue. I know he's a German and I'm supposed to be scared of him, according to some people who say all Germans are devils, but he looks terrified.

'*Hier ist Irland*,' I tell him. '*Wir sind neutral. Du bist hier sicher.*' This is Ireland. We're neutral. You're safe here.

'Ir-land,' he repeats, his voice a croak. He gives a tiny smile. *'Hier ist Irland.'* He closes his eyes for a few seconds, then opens them again. *'Kurt? Hat er überlebt? Und Victor?'* Kurt? Did he make it? And Victor?

Kurt and Victor must be the other airmen.

'He's asking about the other airmen,' I tell Mamó. 'What do I tell him?'

Mamó goes quiet for a moment. Then she says, 'I saw their bodies on the far side of the plane, thrown against the mountain side.' She presses her lips together. 'Poor souls. Best to tell him the truth, that they didn't make it. That he's the only survivor.'

I gulp. That's not easy news to deliver. I look back at him but before I say a word, his eyes well up and tears run down his face. He must have read my expression.

'Kurt!' he cries. *'Kurt! Mein Freund.'* Kurt! My friend.

'Es tut mir wirklich leid,' I tell him. I'm so sorry.

'Grace, we have to get him stable,' Mamó says, kneeling down beside him. 'Can you tell him I'll need to put a tourniquet on his leg to stop the bleeding? Ellen will give him something for the pain.'

I tell him what Mamó said, as best I can, and he nods. Before I move away to let Mamó and Ellen work on him, I squeeze his hand.

'Dir wird alles gut gehen,' I tell him. You're going to be all right.

'Vielen Dank,' he says. Thank you.

I stand with Sibby and watch Mamó and Ellen jump into action. They carefully cut away the bottom of his ripped trouser leg and examine the horrible wound. Mamó says something to

Ellen about preparing the morphine.

'Where did they learn how to do all that?' I ask Sibby.

'Mamó did first-aid training with the Mayo Cumann na mBan. She was in Dublin City Hall during the Easter Rising, running an emergency first-aid clinic. Remember, we did all about it in school?'

'Yes! I had no idea Mamó was involved. She must have some brilliant stories.'

Sibby shrugs. She lowers her voice. 'You'd think. If I was involved in something like that, I'd be full of it. But she never talks about it, ever. I think she found it very upsetting, all the people killed, even children. Better stop talking about it.'

She continues in her normal voice. 'Ellen's always been obsessed with first aid. She used to put bandages on her teddy bears and dolls. Reads all these weird medical textbooks she gets from the library. She has some daft idea about being a doctor.'

'She told me. And I think she'd make a great doctor. Look at her with that needle.'

As we watch, Ellen plunges the needle of a syringe into a tiny glass bottle, sucks up the liquid and then injects it into the airman's thigh. All that practising with the orange clearly worked!

I shudder at the thought of having to push a needle into someone's skin. 'I couldn't do anything like that. Could you? All that blood and stuff.'

"Course I could,' Sibby says firmly, but from the way her face is going pale as we watch I don't think it's true.

Mamó has fixed the tourniquet to the top of the man's thigh and is twisting the material tighter and tighter.

'The bleeding has stopped,' Ellen tells her.

Mamó nods. 'Good. He seems more stable now. Well done, Ellen. Fast work with the morphine. The poor man needed that.'

Ellen gives a big sigh. 'Thanks. That was pretty intense.' But from the brightness in her eyes and the big smile on her face, I think she enjoyed being able to help him. I was right. She *will* make a brilliant doctor.

After a few minutes the man's breathing gets less ragged and his face softens. He opens his eyes, turns his head and looks over at me. He puts his hand on his chest. 'Hans,' he says, then points at me.

'Grace,' I say.

'*Und das Mädchen mit den blauen Augen?*' he asks. And the girl with the blue eyes? I think he means Ellen.

'Ellen,' I say. 'And that's Sibby and Mamó.' I point them out.

He gives a small nod. His eyes close again.

'Is he all right?' I ask Mamó.

'He's just drowsy from the painkiller,' she says. 'Hopefully he'll be fine, thank the Lord.'

I hear the sound of a car or van driving up Fallmore Road and shouts, then the *ding-ding-ding* of a fire engine fills the air.

Dannie and Liam are running towards us, Poppy and Lucky at their heels. 'We're back!' Liam calls over. 'What did we miss?'

'About time,' Mamó says. 'But we have it under control, don't we, ladies? We make a cracking team.'

Sibby nudges me with her shoulder. 'We sure do,' she says.

Does that mean things are fixed between me and Sibby? My heart surges. I do hope so!

Rainbow

Created when sunlight hits a rain droplet and some of
the light is refracted or broken down into different colours

CHAPTER 8

Thursday 11th May, 1944

The following morning at eight o'clock, we're sitting at the breakfast table in the lighthouse when the telephone rings. Flora jumps up to get it. As she walks back into the kitchen, Dad looks at her.

'Very early to be ringing,' he says. 'Who was it? Dunstable?'

'No, the hospital. They want me back in to translate for Hans again.'

Yesterday afternoon, Flora got word that she was needed in Belmullet Hospital immediately. Dad had told the ambulance drivers who looked after Hans that she spoke German, and so she was called in to translate for the doctors.

'Can I come with you?' I ask Flora. 'I can do the weather report before I go.'

'You're supposed to be in school,' Dad says.

'I said they could have the day off,' Flora says. 'They deserve it after being such heroes yesterday.'

'Flora!' Dad says.

She just smiles and shrugs. 'One day off school is hardly going to make any difference.'

'For someone who's so keen on education, that's ripe,' Dad says. 'But I'm not going to argue with you. We've raised two plucky kids, all right.' He reaches over and ruffles Dannie's hair.

'Please can I go to the hospital with you?' I ask Flora again. 'I want to see how Hans is doing. I'll stay beside you, quiet as a mouse.'

Dannie laughs. 'You, quiet?'

'Dannie, don't be unkind,' Flora says. 'Your sister can be quiet when she needs to be. And I have no problem with her coming with me, Tom. It might be good for Hans, in fact. He's anxious, which is understandable, and seeing a friendly face might help.'

'Help?' Dad says. 'He's a German airman, Flora. I would have thought after what the Germans did to your –'

Flora puts up her hand. 'Stop! We talked about this last night. I'm not having any of that. Hans is still a person. And a young one at that. He's probably terrified at the moment, wondering what's going to happen to him after the hospital. Every person on this earth deserves decent treatment, German or not.'

'I suppose,' Dad says, but he doesn't sound very sure. 'If Grace is going to the hospital, I'd better go too. I'll ask Ellen to mind Dannie.'

'I'm nine! I don't need minding,' Dannie says.

'It's more for the dogs than for you,' Dad says. 'You never know what Poppy will get into if she's left alone. And you like Ellen.'

'I suppose,' Dannie grumbles. 'But I'm still old enough to look after myself.'

* * *

'What the hell am I supposed to do with a German prisoner in Blacksod, Tom? If you'll pardon my French, Mrs Devine.' Garda

Collins looks at Dad and then at Flora in bewilderment. Then he looks back down at Hans, who is lying on a hospital trolley, his face very pale.

Garda Collins seems to know Dad well, but I'm not surprised – everyone in Mayo knows Dad. He was on the Mayo GAA team when he was younger, and Mamó told us once he was quite the catch. He broke the hearts of girls all over the county when he married Flora, apparently!

From the guard's brown eyes and round face, he seems kind enough, even though he's rather flustered at the moment. He takes off his flat blue Garda hat and runs a hand through his silver-grey hair before plonking the hat back on his head.

Hans's leg was set last night, but the doctors can't seem to find a room for him, so he's been lying on a trolley in the hallway ever since. His arm is handcuffed to the metal bar along the side of the trolley, which must be uncomfortable, especially with his burns. He's wearing a white cotton hospital gown, and his arms and hands are covered in bandages.

I have a bandage on my right hand too, covering the cuts and burns, and one of my shoulders is sore from shoving Hans out of the cockpit. But it's nothing compared to his injuries.

He's sleeping at the moment, which is good. When we first arrived at Belmullet Hospital today, his whole body was shivering and his face was glistening with sweat so Flora went off to find help. When the doctor arrived and had a look at Hans, he said he was shivering because of the burns, the pain and the shock. He gave him some extra morphine.

'So here's the story,' Garda Collins continues. 'The doctor says there's no hope of a bed for the German lad here in the hospital for at least another few days.'

'Hans,' Flora says. 'That's his name. And I bet there would be a bed if he was an American airman. He's only a boy, for heaven's sake. Can't you sort the doctors out? Where's your compassion? He can't stay chained to a trolley for weeks on end. It's inhumane.' Her eyes are flashing.

Garda Collins looks even more flustered now. He backs away from Flora a little. He takes his hat off again and turns it around and around in his hands.

'No need to get upset, Mrs Devine,' he says. 'I'm only doing my job. It won't be weeks, more like days, as I said. I've been on to my superiors in Dublin and the lad, Hans, is to be interned at the prisoner of war camp in the Curragh. The military officers will come up to transport him as soon as the doctor gives the go-ahead. Until then, he's still my prisoner, and sick or not he has to be kept under lock and key, or at least chained and guarded. Which is a bit of a dilemma. I can't sit here watching him all day. I'll have to put him in the holding cell at the station.'

'Look at him,' Flora says, nodding down at Hans. 'He needs somewhere dry and warm, not noisy and drafty like a cell. The dressings on his burns need to be changed twice a day. The poor boy can barely open his eyes, let alone walk. He's hardly a flight risk. You can't put him in a cell! He's not a criminal.'

Hans stirs a little, his eyelids fluttering but not opening. Then he goes still again.

Garda Collins lowers his voice. 'There's some might say he is, Mrs Devine. Many people don't hold a very high opinion of the

Germans. With good reason. Hitler's a madman. None of us are safe with him around.'

'But Hans isn't –' Flora begins to argue before Dad gives her a look and she stops mid-sentence. I can tell she's dying to say more to Garda Collins, but she's going to let Dad talk now and share her idea, the one they talked about in the car on the way over.

'Harold,' Dad says. 'I understand how difficult all this is for you. I may have a solution to your problem …'

And that is how a German airman comes to be sleeping in our house!

Cirrocumulus

High-level wispy clouds that can look like grains of rice thrown up in the air

CHAPTER 9

Thursday 11th May, 1944

We get home from the hospital around midday. As soon as Dad pulls the car up outside the lighthouse, Dannie comes racing out with Poppy and Lucky barking loudly at his heels. Ellen's just behind him.

'Sorry about the barking,' I say in German to Hans. He is lying along the back seat while I crouch in the footwell. 'They can get a bit excited.'

It wasn't a very comfortable trip for me, especially when we went over bumps, but I didn't mind. It must have been far worse for Hans. The hospital's ambulance was out on a call, and Flora didn't want to wait around for it in case Garda Collins or the doctors changed their minds about letting Hans stay with us.

'Not noisy,' Hans replies in German. 'At home we have seven dogs. And geese. Now they make a racket!'

'Where are you from?' I ask him.

'A village called Gatow. On the outskirts of Berlin. My father is a teacher there.'

'Do you miss it?'

'Yes, very much. I left for college when I was sixteen, just after the war broke out. When I turned eighteen, I had to leave my studies and join the army. That was two years ago, and I haven't been home since.'

Poor Hans! I can't imagine being away from my family and my

home for so long.

Flora opens the back door of the car and calls to Ellen. 'Can you help us get Hans out of the car, Ellen? We need to keep him as comfortable as possible. He's surprisingly heavy for his slim build.'

'Must be all that muscle under his hospital gown,' Ellen says and then instantly goes bright red.

Flora just laughs, ignoring Ellen's pink face. 'Must be.'

Between Flora, Ellen and Dad, they manage to slowly get Hans inside. I help Dannie keep the dogs out from under their feet.

'What's the German doing here?' Dannie asks me as I hold Poppy's collar, keeping her still. I have to do it with my left hand as my right is still tender from the burns.

'Don't call him that. His name is Hans and he's staying with us for a few days while he gets better,' I say.

'Where exactly?' Dannie asks. I must look a bit shifty because he immediately says, 'Not my room? That's not fair! Why isn't he staying in your room?'

'He has to be locked in a room or he can't stay here at all. And your room is the only one on the ground floor with a lock. Mine's up the steps, and he won't be able to manage steps with a broken leg.' Dad and Flora had talked about this on the way home.

'But the lock to my room doesn't even have a key,' Dannie says.

'It does too. Dad and Flora hide it so you won't mess with it and lock yourself in or something daft.'

'I'd never do that!'

I'm about to remind him of the time he locked himself in the toilet when he was five – he went practically hysterical, screaming and kicking at the door, and Flora had to dismantle the whole lock to get him out – but he's way ahead of me.

'That was only once,' he says. 'And I was very small.'

Dannie looks at the kitchen door. It's shut now and everyone else is inside, so it's safe to let the dogs loose. He lets go of Lucky and he walks towards his water bowl sensibly and laps away. When I let Poppy go, she races around the grass like she's chasing a rabbit. Daft thing! At least the gate's firmly closed so she won't be able to run off again.

'If the German's having my room, where am I sleeping then?' Dannie asks. Good question.

'I'm not sure,' I admit. 'Maybe in the store room? There's an old mattress in there.'

'It's full of old junk and spiders.'

He's right. But maybe Flora and Dad will clear it out. As long as they don't ask me to do it. Yuck, spiders! I shiver at the thought of their hairy legs and creepy eyes.

'Let's go in and find out,' I say. 'Make sure Poppy stays out here. She might jump on Hans.'

We open the kitchen door carefully. 'Flora, where's Dannie sleeping?' I ask as soon as we're inside.

She looks up from tending to Hans, who is flopped in the armchair by the stove, his bad leg propped up on the footrest. 'He's sharing with you, Grace,' she says. 'Your bed's easily big enough.'

'What?' I stare at her. 'You never told me that bit. Can't he sleep somewhere else? He snores.'

'I do not!' Dannie says.

'You do too.'

Flora claps her hands together, making Poppy bark outside.

'Enough, the pair of you. And Dannie, the dogs can sleep in with you both as a special treat.'

Dannie smiles and punches the air. 'Yes!' Usually they have to sleep on rugs in front of the stove.

'Flora!' I say. 'Poppy snores too. And she runs in her sleep. I won't get a wink.'

Dad puts his hand on my shoulder. 'If Poppy acts up, you can put them back in the kitchen. Thank you for being so grown up and understanding about it all, Grace.'

'Fine. Dannie can share my bed. But I'm putting a pillow wall down the middle.'

I feel all scratchy inside, but I know I can't keep giving out as Dad has just thanked me for being 'grown up'. It's hardly very grown up to be all huffy, although Mamó often throws huge wobblers when things annoy her. But I guess the rules are different for adults.

And anyway, Ellen's still here. I don't want to be a big baby in front of Ellen. Although I'm not sure she's even listening. She's kneeling beside Hans, carefully adjusting his hospital gown over his bandages.

'Tea, anyone?' Dad asks, looking around the room.

'I think we'd better get Hans to bed first,' Flora says. 'He's starting to look pale and sweaty again.' She looks at her watch. 'He's due more morphine soon. Those burns can't be comfortable. And I have a weather report to deliver in a few minutes too. And I need to polish the lens. I was supposed to do it days ago.'

'Mrs Devine,' Ellen pipes up, 'I know you're really busy with all your work. Can I help with Hans? Give him his morphine?

Change his dressings? I'm well able.'

'Are you sure you have time, Ellen?' Flora asks. 'With your secretarial course? Are you not due back in Dublin soon?'

'I dropped out,' Ellen says. 'It wasn't for me. But please don't tell Mamó or Dad. I haven't told them yet. I'll do it this evening. I'm hoping they will let me apply to medical school.'

'Good for you!' Flora says. 'Well in that case, your help would be most welcome. And I'm sure Hans would enjoy it too. You're far more his age than me. Maybe he could teach you some German if he's feeling up to it. It would keep him busy and his brain engaged.'

Ellen smiles. 'Maybe he could. And I could teach him some English.'

'Even better idea,' Flora says. 'It might prove useful in the prisoner of war camp.'

'Is that where he's off to next?' Ellen asks.

Flora nods. 'Yes, in Kildare. By all accounts, it's not the worst of places. I've heard they even play football matches, the Allies against the Germans. It will keep him safe for the rest of the war, anyway.'

Dad mutters something rude about Germans not deserving to be safe, but Flora ignores him. 'Right,' she continues, 'better get that weather report done. Grace, you can do the next one if that's OK. First, I need you to explain what's happening to Hans – about moving him to his room and Ellen helping to nurse him. Dannie, you come outside and help me read the instruments for the weather report.'

'But I don't know how to do them all,' Dannie says.

'I know,' Flora says, 'which is why you're about to learn. All hands on deck and all that.'

'Oh, before you go, Flora, I forgot to tell you there was a phone call,' Ellen says. 'Gentleman asking to speak to Grace. I told him to try calling back later. Said he was from *The Irish Daily*, no less.' Ellen raises her eyebrows at me. 'Had a very la-di-da voice. I wrote the number on the notebook beside the phone.'

'Are you sure he said me?' I ask her.

Ellen smiles. '"The girl who spotted the crash and saved the German." That's you, isn't it?'

'I suppose it is.'

'He wanted to interview you,' Ellen says. 'For a newspaper report.'

'Wow!' Dannie says. 'You'll be famous. Don't forget to mention me.'

'Can't you do it, Flora?' I say. 'What on earth am I going to say to a posh *Irish Daily* reporter?' My stomach butterflies at the thought of it.

'You'll be grand, pet,' Flora says. 'Just be yourself and tell him what happened. It's not rocket science. Far easier than phoning in a weather report, and you've been doing those beautifully. But don't say a thing about Hans being here with us. It might not go down too well with Dublin folk. Best to keep it to ourselves. Now, chop, chop, Dannie. We'd better get moving.'

'I'll talk to Hans, then phone the reporter before I chicken out,' I say.

'That's the spirit, Grace!' Flora says, patting me on the back. '"Once more unto the breach", as Shakespeare said!'

Dad sighs. 'She's talking to a reporter, Flora, not storming a

German fort or something.'

Flora gives Dad a wink. 'That can be Grace's next job.'

'Honestly, Flora, for a pacifist you do say the darndest things at times,' Dad says.

Flora just grins. It's good to see her smile and joke. Helping Hans seems to have put her in good spirits. I hope it lasts.

I walk towards Hans and kneel down beside Ellen to talk to him.

'Hello, Hans,' I say. 'How are you feeling?'

He gives a tiny shrug. 'I've been better. But I am grateful to be here and for all your family are doing for me. And Ellen, of course. She is very kind.'

'And very pretty.' Oops, it's out of my mouth before I can stop it.

He smiles. 'Yes. Very. But don't tell her I said so.' He gives me a wink.

From the way Ellen is looking at Hans, her cheeks turning pink again, I think she's worked it out!

Cirrostratus

A pale, wispy cloud made up of ice crystals that can look like
thin stripes in the sky

CHAPTER 10

Thursday 11th May, 1944

I dial the number Ellen had taken down for the reporter. It takes a little longer than usual as I have to do it with my left fingers. Then I press the telephone receiver to my ear, the black bakelite cool against the edge of my cheek.

'Mr Oscar Woodworth speaking,' a plummy voice rings out. 'How may I help you?'

'It's Grace Devine from Blacksod. You rang looking for me.' I can hear a slight wobble in my voice and my hands are shaking. *Don't be silly*, I tell myself. Flora's right, it's no different to a weather report. Tell him the facts.

'Ah, yes, Miss Devine. Bingo! If we're quick, I think we still have time to catch tomorrow's front page. Let's get cracking. I believe you live in Blacksod Lighthouse, is that right?'

'That's right, yes.'

'Charming, charming. With your parents and brother?'

'Yes, Dannie. He's nine. And our dogs, Lucky and Poppy.'

'Dogs?' He seems to perk up at this. 'Good hunters?'

Hunters? I'm not sure what he means by this. 'They're Labradors,' I say.

'Ah, retrievers, excellent, excellent. So tell me about this plane crash. You spotted smoke, I believe. Start from the beginning. I'll be taking down what you say in my best shorthand. You might hear the odd scribble or pause as I do so.'

'All right,' I say, although when he talks about taking notes it makes me even more nervous. What if I say something daft? I'll have to be as careful as I can. Watch every word. My hands are starting to go clammy, and I clutch the telephone receiver even tighter.

I can hear the shuffle of papers. 'And I believe there was a Miss Ellen Lavelle involved? A bit of a looker, if my sources are to be trusted.'

'She's here,' I blurt out. I manage not to say 'nursing Hans'. I know I can't mention that bit. 'She's our neighbour,' I say instead.

He gives a short laugh that sounds like a seal cough. 'Excellent, excellent. Two birds with one stone and all that. And your parents don't mind you being in the paper?'

'No, as long –' I cut myself off. *As long as I don't talk about Hans,* I was about to say. *Grace,* I tell myself sternly. *Concentrate!* 'As long as I tell the truth,' I say instead.

'Very good. Always the best option,' he says. 'Unless it gets in the way of a good story.' He barks out another laugh. 'Although don't quote me on that. Only joking, naturally. Now, tell me what happened yesterday, from when you first spotted the smoke.'

'So I was up a ladder fixing the anemometer – that's an instrument for measuring wind speed – when I spotted smoke coming from Fallmore Hill ...'

I tell him the whole story: running to the Lavelles' house, Poppy finding Hans, Ellen and Mamó and their first aid, everything. Right up to when Hans reached the hospital.

'What a great story!' Mr Woodworth says. 'And he's in Belmullet Hospital, this Nazi. Hans something or other?'

91

'Hans Holban. H-O-L-B-A-N.' I spell out the name carefully so Mr Woodworth will get it right. For some reason, it feels important. Flora's right. Nazi or no Nazi, Hans is a person, just like everyone else.

'Going to survive, is he, this Hans person?'

'Yes. He's got bad burns and a broken leg and ribs, but he'll survive.' I'm careful not to add anything else.

'And he'll be taken to the internment camp in the Curragh once he can travel, is that correct?'

'Yes,' I say simply.

'Sounds like you were a real hero, Grace. Saved his life. Anything you'd like to add?'

'Can you make sure to mention my brother Dannie, please?'

'Of course, of course. Anything else?'

'No, that's it.' At this stage I'm desperately keen to get off the telephone in case I say something I'm not supposed to say. My stomach is in knots as it is.

'Wonderful, wonderful. Could I have a quick word with Miss Lavelle? I'd love to get a few quotes from her. It will give some colour to the whole piece.'

'No problem,' I say. 'I'll go and get her for you.'

As I walk into the kitchen, I have a feeling I've left something out … but I can't for the life of me think what it is.

'Ellen, the reporter would like a word with you,' I tell her. She's still sitting beside Hans, although he's asleep now.

'Me?' Ellen looks less delighted than I thought she would. 'Do I have to?' She looks over at Dad who is sitting at the kitchen table, his hands wrapped around a mug of tea.

'Not if you don't want to,' Dad says. 'I can tell him you've just left.'

'Would you, Mr Devine? I'd be most grateful.'

I stare at Dad. I hadn't thought that was an option, saying no to an *Irish Daily* reporter. Flora encouraged me to do the interview. I feel stupid. I wish I'd had the guts to say no like Ellen. Too late now!

'Leave it to me,' Dad says, walking out of the kitchen.

'You all right, Grace?' Ellen says. 'You look a little surprised. I know Sibby would love to be in the newspaper, but I'm not Sibby.'

Sibby! My veins fill with ice. I haven't left something out, I've left *someone* out. Surely I mentioned her when I was talking about going to the Lavelles' house and dashing to the crash together? Or did I? I was so nervous and flustered I honestly can't remember. She's going to kill me if I didn't! I run towards the office and almost collide with Dad.

'Woah, Grace! What's got into you?' he says.

'I need to ring him back. Mr Woodworth. I left something out. Something vital.'

He looks at me for a moment and then nods. 'If it's important to you, Grace, you can ring him back.'

'Thanks, Dad.'

I ring the *Irish Daily* number again, but it's engaged. I try again and again, but when someone finally does answer, a woman, she says Mr Woodworth's not available.

But maybe it will all be ok. The Lavelles don't take *The Irish Daily* – I know because I sometimes help Dad deliver the papers during the school holidays. Ellen's not going to be in the paper, so maybe Sibby won't even see it. Maybe I'm worrying about nothing.

As Flora says, 'Today's news, tomorrow's chip paper.' Let's hope she's right!

* * *

At seven that evening, I ring in the weather report for Flora.

I recognise Maureen's voice as soon as she says, 'Hello, this is Dunstable 2100. How may I help you?'

'Good evening, this is Blacksod Weather Station, County Mayo, with the 19:00 hours weather report.'

'Ah, 'tis yourself, Grace. How are things in Blacksod?'

'Good, thanks. And you?'

'Not too bad. Busy. Long hours. I'm a bit tired today, but the war won't win itself and all that. Better get cracking with the readouts.'

'Of course.' I give her the readings from the different instruments. Wind direction and speed, temperature, rainfall, air pressure and finally cloud coverage.

'Visibility good. Cloud coverage high and fast-moving uncinus,' I tell her.

She goes quiet for a moment. 'Uncinus? It's not on my list, Grace. Are you sure you have that right?'

'Sorry, just put down "cirrus". When the cirrus clouds look like hooks in the sky, they're uncinus, you see. But don't worry about it. Cirrus is close enough.'

Maureen gives a laugh. 'You're right! Uncinus, of course. My met studies are coming back to me. I used to call them unicorn clouds because the ends look like curved unicorn horns. Sounds like it's fine weather in Blacksod this evening, lucky you. Talk to you tomorrow, Grace. Keep safe.'

'You too, Maureen.'

Nimbostratus

Low, depressing cloud cover that blocks the sun and
produces lots of rain

CHAPTER 11

Friday 12th May, 1944

I'm woken the following morning by someone jumping on my legs.

'Dannie!' I cry out. 'What are you doing?' I sit up a bit and swipe at him with my hand, but it lands on fur.

I open my eyes and groan. It's Poppy, sitting on my eiderdown, gazing at me, her brown eyes sparkling in the gloom. She licks my cheek and I wipe the sticky saliva away. It took me ages to get to sleep last night. My hand was a bit sore, plus I was worrying about Sibby and what I had or hadn't said to Mr Woodworth. I tried not to think about it, but I couldn't help it. I'm in no mood for Poppy's nonsense this morning.

'Get off me, you stupid dog,' I mutter, pushing her off the bed. She lands on Dannie, who is sleeping on a mattress on my floor. He kept kicking me, even with the pillow wall between us, so I pulled the mattress out of the store room for him and the dogs to sleep on.

Dannie opens his eyes for a second, puts his arms around Poppy's neck and pulls her against him. 'Don't be mean to her, Grace,' he says. 'Go back to sleep, Poppy.'

But Poppy's wide awake now and raring to go. She barks, setting Lucky off.

'Shush, both of you,' I say. 'OK, OK, we'll get up.'

Sighing, I drag myself up and open the curtains and then the shutters. The sun is already beaming down on the still water of

Blacksod Bay, making it shine like blue satin. It's hard to be cross with Poppy on such a beautiful morning.

'What time is it?' Dannie asks.

I look at my wristwatch. 'Ten to six.'

'Six?' He gives a loud moan. 'That's too early to get up! Close the shutters, will you? I want to go back to sleep.'

'No, you're taking the dogs outside. Otherwise they'll wake up Flora and Dad with their barking. And Hans.'

'I'd forgotten about Hans.' He pauses. 'What day is it?'

I'm so tired I have to think. 'Friday.'

'Do we have to go to school?'

'I guess so. Dad will make us.'

'And you're going to be in the paper today. I'm gonna be famous, famous.' He starts singing 'Follow the Yellow Brick Road' to himself. It's his favourite song from *The Wizard of Oz*. What it has to do with being famous, I have no idea. Strange how my little brother's mind works!

'Actually I think I will get up,' he says. While he sings his way out the bedroom door, down the stairs and into the kitchen to bring the dogs out, I take a few deep breaths, trying to make myself feel less nervous. *It will all be fine*, Grace, I tell myself. *Sibby will be fine, school will be fine. It will all be fine, fine, fine …*

* * *

Although I told Dad not to, at half past six he insists on driving the whole way to the post office to get an early copy of *The Irish Daily* to read over breakfast. I'm sitting in the kitchen waiting for him to return. Flora is checking on Hans, and Dannie is chomping on a piece of toast, giving his crusts to the dogs under the table.

Flora walks back into the kitchen. 'How is Hans?' I ask her.

'He says he had a much better night than in the hospital. Managed to get some rest. But he's still very weak. I've given him his medicine and a few sips of broth. I expect he'll sleep for most of the day. You can visit him after school.'

Dad walks in waving *The Irish Daily* in front of him like it's a gold medal he's won in a race. 'Not every day my first born is in a national newspaper.' He looks at me. 'Are you all right, Grace? You seem a bit pale.' He puts his hand on my forehead. 'You don't seem hot. Do you feel all right?'

'Not really. My stomach feels like it's full of frogs.'

He gives a laugh. 'Excited about this, I'm sure. Front page too. Above the fold. Look.'

He jabs his finger at the newspaper. There's a large black and white photograph of the plane crash and to the right of it, Ellen's head in a round bubble. I'm confused. Ellen didn't even talk to Mr Woodworth. What's her smiling face doing there?

'I'll pop it on the table, shall I?' he says, unfolding it on the wood and smoothing down the middle crease with his hands. 'Let's all have a read together. I see they managed to find a photograph of Ellen.'

Flora peers at the paper. 'Looks like an old school one, from what she's wearing.'

She's right. Ellen's dressed in her old Our Lady's pinafore over a long-sleeved school shirt.

I read the headline above the photograph – 'Local Beauty Saves the Day' – then I quickly scan the piece for the only thing that really matters to me, Sibby's name. I spot lots of names in the small black print: Dannie, Kathleen Lavelle – that's Mamó – Liam, Ellen, more Ellen, Hans, even Poppy and Lucky, but no Sibby. Not one mention of Sibby. Yikes!

Then I go back to the start and read it properly.

Seventeen-year-old local beauty Miss Ellen Lavelle and her Cumann na mBan grandmother, Mrs Kathleen Lavelle, saved the life of a German airman when his Junkers 88 meteorology aeroplane crashed in Blacksod, Co Mayo, on Wednesday afternoon.

The daughter of the Blacksod Lighthouse Keeper, Mr Thomas Devine, raised the alarm about the crash. 'I saw smoke coming from one of the fields on the side of the hill,' Miss Grace Devine (12) explained. 'I grabbed my mother's first-aid bag and ran to the Lavelles' house to get help.'

Miss Devine then found the airman – Mr Hans Holban – in the crashed plane with the help of her dog, Poppy. She bravely dragged him out of the cockpit where he was trapped. The Lavelle ladies took on the role of first aiders while Dannie Devine and Liam Lavelle went for help …

The rest of the article is all about Ellen, how she saved Hans's life by stopping the bleeding from his leg and how if there was a Miss Belmullet competition, her flaxen locks and cornflower blue eyes would surely win the title. And then Mr Woodworth goes and writes it: 'the face of a matinee star'.

I wince. Sibby's not going to like that! I read on. There are some quotes from a lady from Cumann na mBan about their excellent first-aid training, and from Father McRory about how he always knew Ellen was a wonder, even as a young child. 'She's destined for great things, that Ellen Lavelle' is the final quote.

I blow out my breath.

'Overwhelming, isn't it, Grace?' Dad says. 'Seeing your name in print like that. Reflecting on the danger you were in, all of you. But that journalist is right, you were a real heroine.'

'Thanks, Dad,' I murmur. 'I'm not feeling very well. Can I go back to bed?'

'Don't you want to show this to all your friends?' He nods down at the paper.

I shake my head.

'What is it, Grace?' Flora asks. She's looking at me carefully. 'Have they misquoted you in some way? You don't look happy.'

I sigh. I may as well say it out loud. There's nothing I can do now and soon everyone is going to know. 'They left Sibby out.'

'I'm sure she won't mind,' Dad says.

I look down at my hands. 'She'll mind,' I say quietly.

'Sibby wants to be famous,' Dannie says. 'She's always going on about it.'

'Dannie's right,' I say. 'She wants to be a Hollywood actress.'

Dad says, 'Hollywood? A girl from Blacksod? That's a good one.' He chuckles away to himself until Flora glares at him to stop.

'Maureen O'Hara is famous and she's Irish,' I say, repeating what Sibby told me.

'Fair point,' Dad says. 'Sorry, I didn't mean to be unkind.'

'Did you mention Sibby to the journalist?' Flora asks me.

I shake my head. 'I don't think so. He kept asking me about Ellen. I forgot about Sibby.'

'Ellen's a beautiful young woman,' Flora says. 'Often people don't see past that, like this journalist. He had a particular story he wanted to tell – the one in the headline, 'Local Beauty Saves the Day' – and he told it. But that's hardly your fault, Grace. Come on, chop, chop. You both need to get ready for school.'

'School?' I say. 'Do I have to?'

Dad nods. 'You had yesterday off. You can't miss another day. What would Miss Waldron think?'

'She'd understand,' I say. 'I'm begging you. Don't make me go in today.' I look at Flora and press my hands together. 'Please?'

Dad gives Flora a stern look.

'Your dad's right,' Flora says. 'Talk to Sibby, explain you didn't mean to leave her out. She'll understand.'

'Have you met Sibby Lavelle?' I ask. I give a loud groan. 'You're sending me to the lions, both of you.'

Dad smiles. 'Grace, don't be so melodramatic. It will be fine, you'll see.'

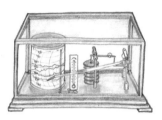

Cumulonimbus

Large storm clouds that produce heavy rain
and sometimes hail

CHAPTER 12

Friday 12th May, 1944

My heart is hammering in my chest when I call for Sibby to walk to school with me. I'm not expecting her to be pleased to see me. Dannie's just behind me, calling for Liam.

Ellen opens the door. 'Liam!' she shouts down the hallway. 'Dannie's here for you.'

Liam dashes past me, his brown leather school satchel over his shoulder. He joins Dannie on the path, and they disappear together in a rush of sticky-up hair and tumble-down knee socks.

Ellen gives me a smile, but it doesn't reach her eyes. 'Sibby's gone on ahead again,' she says.

'Did she see the paper this morning?' I ask her.

She nods wordlessly.

'Is it bad?' I ask. 'Sibby, I mean?'

Ellen winces. 'She went ballistic after she'd read it. Called me a liar and a traitor and a glory-hogger.' She gives a little laugh. 'Great word, I think she made it up. Said I'd ruined her chance at fame. I told her I didn't even speak to the journalist, but she didn't believe me. Dad rang the editor about using my photograph without permission, but it was in the local paper last year and they took it from there. There's nothing we can do about it. I'm not happy though.'

I can feel my cheeks flame bright red. 'I'm so sorry,' I say. 'I should never have talked to that journalist.'

'It's not your fault, Grace. He would have run the story regardless. And look, he said nice things about us both. Most people would be delighted by the attention.'

'But not you,' I point out.

'No,' she says simply. 'Not me.'

'Is there anything I can do?' I ask her. 'About Sibby, I mean?'

She shakes her head. 'Just ride it out. She'll have to do something else interesting or brave – get in the paper another way. Be the first girl on the moon or something. The scientists believe it will happen one day. Space travel in giant rockets. Sooner than we think.'

Despite everything, I smile. Trust Ellen to know something like that. 'Thanks, Ellen. I might see you later at the house.'

'You will. I'll be over to help your mum with Hans once breakfast is cleared away. How is he this morning?'

'Flora said he managed to get some sleep last night. And he ate a bit of broth.'

'Good.' She pauses for a moment. 'Grace, I know Sibby can be difficult sometimes but you two have been friends for a long time. You've been through a lot together and a friendship like that is very special. You're good for each other. Hang in there. She'll get over it.'

'I hope so.'

'And the journalist was right. You were very brave pulling Hans out like that.'

'Sibby was brave too.' I swallow down a sob. I feel very emotional this morning. It's all getting to me, I think – the crash, not sleeping well, Sibby …'

Ellen smiles at me, a genuine, eye-twinkling smile this time. 'Grace, it's going to be all right, I promise. Just keep moving forwards, like a shark. You know some species of shark die if they stop swimming?'

'I did not know that. Thanks, Ellen.'

She pulls me in for a hug. It's a surprise – she's not generally the huggy type – but a nice surprise. She smells of fresh toast and strawberry jam. 'Grace, you're one of a kind,' she says. 'I know you'd fight lions for my sister, and in her heart, she knows it too. Never change. Now get to school. Those facts won't learn themselves.' She pulls away and pushes me gently out the door.

* * *

By breaktime the sun is beaming down and some of the older girls, including me, have flopped under the hawthorn tree beside the schoolhouse to eat our lunch. The younger children – Miss Murphy's infant class – go home before lunch. I don't have the energy for playing football today.

I tried talking to Sibby earlier, before school started, but she was being really weird.

'Grace, I'm sorry, I can't talk to you anymore,' she said as we walked to our desks. She made a big deal of looking all around her and then leant towards me and whispered, 'It's too dangerous.'

'Dangerous? What are you talking about, Sibby?' I said, but she turned away and started asking Maria Kennedy how she did her ringlets. This was a first. She usually calls Maria a ninny.

'I'm sick of this stupid war,' Maria is saying now, under the tree. 'I went to the shop yesterday to get bullseyes and they only had those horrid sticky brown sweets that taste like cod liver oil. And

Da says we can only take the Ford out on Sundays as there's not enough petrol to run it every day, 'cos of rationing and all. And he makes me feed the cows these smelly nut things in the shed every morning before school.'

'Why don't they eat grass in the fields like normal cows?' Sibby asks.

'The government says everyone has to grow crops instead, on account of the Emergency. Look! The farm work is ruining my moon manicure. All the film stars have moon nails, like Bette Davis.' Maria shows Sibby her hand. Then she holds the tips of her fingers up for everyone to inspect.

Moon manicure? Maria's eleven! Yes, I can see big white moons at the skin edge of her nails, but the tops are short, stubby and square. 'Hardly film star nails …' I snort under my breath. It must have been louder than I'd intended as Sibby is staring at me.

'It's fine for you, Grace, with your fancy smancy shop biscuits and extra diesel,' Sibby says. 'The Emergency is just sliding off you. We know where you're getting the fuel from. The Brits! Your family are all British spies. Helping the Allies. Giving out secret information on the telephone. Saving the German airman was just a cover-up, wasn't it? To throw the Nazis off your family's scent.'

What is she blathering on about now? 'Secret information?' I say. 'Are you talking about the weather reports, Sibby?'

Her eyes narrow. 'Are you sure they're weather reports? I think you're sending secret coded messages about German planes to London. I've seen you watching the sky with those binoculars of yours. We're supposed to be neutral, not helping the Allies. You're going to get us all in serious trouble.'

'I am sure, in fact, Miss Smarty Pants,' I say. 'But I'm not going to waste my time explaining what a barometer and air pressure readings are to someone with a brain the size of a peanut whose only obsession is being famous. As if that's going to happen. And don't tell me you starred as Holy Mary last Christmas. Hollywood directors are hardly going to discover you in the St Patrick's School nativity play. You're just annoyed with me about the newspaper article. You wanted to be the star of it, not Ellen. And have your photograph on the front page. Admit it!'

There's a stony silence for a moment before Maria gives a nervous giggle. The girls have stopped looking at me and have all turned to look at Sibby, waiting for her reply. It's like they're watching a tennis match and I've just lobbed a high ball at her.

'It's got nothing to do with that,' Sibby says, glaring at me. 'And I know all about barometers, thank you very much. We have a brand-new scientific barometer in the study, and I know exactly how to read it. It's all the way from Glasgow. Bet yours isn't from Glasgow.'

Their heads all turn my way again at this smash ball from Sibby. I'd forgotten that Sibby's dad is interested in the weather. He runs the canning factory now, but he used to be the captain of a big fishing boat.

'You'd better watch yourself, Grace Devine,' she continues. 'Everyone knows your mam's secretly helping the Brits 'cos she's one of them. She's a spy and she's going to get us all blown up by a Nazi bomber.'

I stare at her. 'That's ridiculous. She's not a spy, and no-one's going to bomb Blacksod. It's a small village in the middle of nowhere.'

'I don't mean the village, I mean the lighthouse, you ninny. The Jerries shot at Blackrock Island Lighthouse last year, and they might bomb your lighthouse next and accidentally kill us too. And it will be all your mam's fault for being a British spy.'

Darn it, Sibby's right. The Germans did try to bomb the lighthouse on Blackrock Island, but they didn't succeed. I heard Dad and Flora talking about it. I blocked it out of my mind as it was too scary to think about.

Sibby's always been good at arguing, too good. My brain is frozen, and I can't think of a single comeback. My skin feels all prickly with annoyance. She's not usually this mean. That newspaper article must have really, really annoyed her.

'Flora's not a bloody spy!' I snap. 'You shut your mouth, Sibby Lavelle!' Before I know it, I've leant over and given her a shove. From the way she's holding her shoulder and screaming the place down, you'd think I'd landed a knock-out punch in the gob.

'What's going on out here?' Miss Waldron appears beside us, face like a disgusted umpire, wiping her fingers on her green linen skirt and leaving chalky white stripes. 'Sibby, why are you wailing like a banshee?' she asks.

'Grace hit me.'

'Liar!' I say. 'I pushed you and only a bit. Don't exaggerate.'

Miss Waldron gives a long, drawn-out sigh, like air being let out of a tyre. 'Grace, take your lunch inside, please.'

'But Miss,' I protest, 'she called Flora a British spy.'

Sibby makes her eyes go all blinky and innocent. 'I said no such thing. And even if her mam is a spy, Grace can't go around hitting people, can she, Miss?'

Miss Waldron pulls herself up, which makes her look even more statuesque. She's taller than most men in Blacksod, but it never seems to bother her. I love that about her.

'Sibby, for heaven's sake,' she says, 'Mrs Devine is not a British spy, and you mustn't spread such dangerous nonsense. Please save your vivid imagination for English composition. But you're right, physical violence is not acceptable. Grace will do some lines – "I must not push people in school". Does that satisfy your deeply embedded sense of justice, Sibby?'

Sibby nods. 'Yes, Miss. She should write "hit people" though, not "push".'

Miss Waldron stares at her for a long moment and Sibby's freckled cheeks flush red then white. '"Push" is fine, Miss,' she stammers.

'Good. And I never want to hear silly prattle about Mrs Devine again, understand?'

'Yes, Miss,' Sibby says. 'I'll make sure no-one calls Mrs Devine a British spy even though she's from Scotland.'

'You do that, Sibby,' Miss Waldron says with a crisp nod. 'Mrs Devine has lived here longer than you've been alive. It doesn't matter where she's from, you can't go around calling her a spy. As you were, ladies. Back to your talk of moon manicures and all the rest.'

As we walk towards the schoolhouse, I wonder how Miss Waldron knows about the moon manicures. 'Were you listening through the window, Miss?' I ask her.

'I'd never eavesdrop on my students, Grace. How could you even suggest such a thing?' She gives me a wink.

Once inside the schoolroom, Miss Waldron turns to me and says in a lower and much kinder voice, 'I know Sibby can be annoying and says some ridiculous things, but you must rise above it, Grace. I thought you two had made up again. And you certainly can't hit *her*, of all children, understand? Her father is Chairman of the St Patrick's School board. It's a surefire way of getting suspended or even expelled. I want to keep you in school so you can apply for the scholarship for the secondary school in Castlebar, and Sibby's dad will have to agree. And I'd like you to consider going on to university after that, Trinity College Dublin, like your mother. Would you like that?'

'I think so, but I know Dad's not keen on me studying in Dublin. He thinks it's too far away. Did you go to university, Miss?'

'Yes, in Dublin. I studied science in University College Dublin, not far from your mother's college. Afterwards, I took a teacher training course in Limerick. Not my idea, but there you go. Not many jobs out there for women scientists in Mayo, I'm afraid, and I wanted to live and work near my mother and my family. It is getting better for women, but not quickly enough if you ask me.'

'Don't you like being a teacher?'

'What a question, Grace. Always with the questions.' Smiling, she hands me the blackboard cleaner. The grey felt is so hard and worn down it looks like slate. 'Now clean the right-hand side of the board, please, and write your lines,' she says. 'That way we won't waste any paper on them.'

'But *lines*, Miss? At least give me a useful job like sharpening pencils or correcting the maths books. And I'm not sure I'd be able for many lines anyway. My hand still isn't great. Although Flora says I need to stretch it gently and get back to doing things.' I hold up my bandaged hand.

'I'm sorry, I'd forgotten about that. And you're quite right. Lines are an awful waste of time. Next lesson is geography. Could you manage to draw the outline of a volcano on the board?'

'I'll give it a go.'

'Good girl. But don't hurt yourself. Stop if it gets sore. Make sure it's nice and big. I'll be asking the class to name the parts, so put them all in. Your diagrams are far better than mine. Perhaps you'll be a geographer or a scientist one day. You have one of the sharpest brains of any child I've ever taught in St Patrick's.'

'Even Ellen Lavelle?' I ask.

She laughs. 'I'd say you're about equal when it comes to science, but your grasp of languages is extraordinary. Never tell anyone I said so. I don't like to be seen to be playing favourites.' She hands me a wooden box of coloured chalks and a geography textbook with a faded red cover.

'Thank you, Miss. I won't.'

She also hands me the glittering treasure of her words: 'one of the sharpest brains'. Imagine! As sharp as Ellen's! Flora is always telling me I'm super smart, but hearing it from my teacher, that's different. If only I could use my sharp brain to work out how to stay friends with Sibby.

It's as if Miss Waldron can read my mind. She looks at me for a moment then says, 'I'm not going to give you another lecture about friendship, Grace.'

Poor Miss Waldron has seen more than her fair share of fireworks between me and Sibby over the years. Like the tantrum Sibby threw in class last December when I voted for Albert Cosgrove's artwork instead of hers for the front cover of the Christmas newsletter. Sibby's a brilliant actress but Albert's the best artist in the class, and everyone knows it, even Sibby. He's nice too, quiet, keeps to himself. He deserved to win.

'I'm not going to tell you that friendship is like a garden that has to be watered,' she continues. 'Or that it's like the weather – it has storms as well as sunny days.'

'Pretty stormy today,' I say, and she smiles.

'But I will say this: A good friend is worth all the hurricanes the world can throw at you. Don't give up. You need each other. Your honesty is commendable, Grace, but would it hurt to say sorry once in a while? And to show that you really are sorry?'

'That's so unfair! I tried to apologise but she never gave me a chance.'

'Keep trying. Sniping at her isn't going to make things any better.'

'What about *her*? Spreading lies about Flora like that.' I take a piece of chalk in my fingers and start to draw the outline of a volcano on the board. I press so hard the chalk snaps. I pick the broken piece off the floor and stare at it.

'No-one believes that nonsense,' Miss Waldron says. 'She's just lashing out because she's hurt at being left out. The whole village saw that article this morning. It's the talk of the town. All the parents were gabbing about it when they dropped off the infants to Miss Murphy. It can't be easy having a sister like Ellen taking all the limelight. Especially one who doesn't even care about the limelight, when you care about it so very much.' She gives a laugh. 'I said no lecture. I just can't help myself.' She tilts her head and looks at my drawing. 'Good start. It'll all work itself out, Grace. Calm after the storm and all that.'

But Miss Waldron is wrong. There's another storm brewing. This one much closer to home ...

Altocumulus

Mid-level clouds which form clumps or rolls

CHAPTER 13

Saturday 13th May, 1944

'Visibility, good,' I say into the telephone receiver. 'Cloud cover, altocumulus. Looks like a sky full of cotton wool balls. But the weather's definitely breaking. It feels different out there.'

'Are you all right, Grace?' Maureen asks. 'Your voice is quieter today, flatter. Anything wrong?'

'Just some stuff going on at school. I won't let it get in the way of the weather reports.'

'Take care of yourself. *Slán agus beannacht leat.*'

'You speak Irish, Maureen?'

'I do indeed! It's a great way to confuse the Germans too.'

I give a laugh. 'Do they listen to our weather reports, do you think?'

'They listen to everything, Grace. This line is protected, though, so never you mind about that. Have a good day. I hope tomorrow is a bit brighter for you.'

'Thanks, Maureen. *Slán agus go n-éirí leat!*'

* * *

When I come back from walking Lucky and Poppy, I spot Flora in the garden. The office rug is strung up on the washing line and she's thumping it hard with the wooden carpet beater. *Whomp!*

Whomp! Whomp! Tiny dirt and dust particles are swirling in the air.

I call over to her, but she ignores me and keeps thrashing the rug. She seems to be muttering something under her breath. Very odd.

I go inside. Dad's at the kitchen table, tucking into some bread and ham.

'What's up with Flora?' I ask him.

He stops eating and passes me a piece of paper. 'This came through the door earlier.'

I read it:

Mr and Mrs Devine,

Your presence is required at a public meeting at the Blacksod Community Hall to discuss the NAZI PRISONER OF WAR who is being sheltered in the lighthouse, which as you know is a PUBLIC BUILDING.

4pm, Saturday 13th May, 1944

'Who's it from?' I ask.

Dad shrugs. 'Good question. It doesn't say, but I think we can guess. It looks like Father McRory's handwriting. He likes to be at the centre of everything in Blacksod. I thought the capital letters were a bit unnecessary myself. Anyway, your mother is understandably not happy. Hence she's taking it out on the rug.'

'Are you going to the meeting?'

'I guess we don't have much choice. We've been summoned by the powers that be.'

'Then I'm going too.'

Dad shakes his head. 'It's not suitable for children, Grace. Lord knows what will be said.'

'It's my fault Hans is here,' I say.

'I wouldn't use the word "fault", Grace. It was a magnificent thing you did, saving Hans like that. But you have a point. I'll see what your mum says.'

* * *

We walk through the door of the community hall at exactly four o'clock, Dad, Flora, Dannie and me. Flora let us both come in the end.

'Having children there might help, in fact,' she said when Dad asked her about it. 'They have more sense than most adults, and it might calm people down a bit.'

There's a big crowd in the hall – the whole village seems to be here. I spot Mamó, Mr Lavelle and Sibby up near the front. Ellen's at our house keeping an eye on Hans.

Father McRory is on the stage, sitting behind a trestle table with Mrs Reilly, Mattie's mother, on one side and Mr Kennedy, Maria's father, on the other.

'The usual suspects,' Flora whispers to Dad.

'Ah, here they are,' Father McRory says when he spots us. 'The Devines, right on time. Up to the front, please, we have chairs reserved for you.' He gestures at the front row.

Dad looks at Flora, who rolls her eyes and gives a small nod. We make our way to the chairs and sit down. My fingers are tingling with nerves. All these people. What are they going to say to Flora? Is she in trouble? Will Hans be sent away?

Father McRory coughs. Then he claps his hands together to settle the crowd, like we're in infant class. He says, 'We're here today by request of several members of the community who are, shall I say, a bit concerned at a certain matter.'

Mrs Reilly stares at him and nods, as if to say, 'Go on, Father.'

'The matter of a, well, a, how shall I say it …?' he continues.

'Nazi, Father,' Mrs Reilly says. 'He's a Nazi.'

Father McRory nods. 'Yes, well, I suppose that is true. The matter of a *Nazi* in our midst.'

There's silence for a second and then Flora stands up. 'His name is Hans Holban,' she says firmly. 'He's not in our midst, he's under lock and key. And he will remain so until he is transferred to the Prisoner of War camp at the Curragh, as agreed by Garda Collins from Belmullet Garda Station, a man known to all of you here today. It's all above board, Father. There's nothing to worry about or discuss.'

'But until he is in the camp, we are all in grave danger, Mrs Devine, can't you see that?' Mrs Reilly says. 'He may have you wrapped around his little German finger, but not us. Oh no! Those Nazis are evil murderers. What if he kills you in your sleep and comes for us next, eh?'

There's a squeal from someone. It sounds suspiciously like Sibby. I turn around to look but she stares back at me, all innocent big cow eyes.

Flora's mouth twitches and she pulls herself up straight. Like Miss Waldron, she's taller than a lot of the men in the hall. 'This young man, who is just twenty, never wanted to be in the war in the first place,' she says. 'He's a meteorologist, a weather scientist, not a soldier. He's covered in burns from head to toe and he has a badly broken leg and several broken ribs. He's barely conscious. He's not capable of getting out of bed, let alone killing anyone.'

'Why are you so fond of these Nazis then, eh?' Mrs Reilly asks, her eyes narrowing. 'I would have thought you'd hate them. What with your brother and all. Alfred, wasn't it? Whose side are you on, Mrs Devine? The Nazis or the Allies?'

I hear Flora take a deep breath. It can't be easy hearing Alfie's name brought into it like that. Dad puts his hand on her arm. 'You all right, Flora?' he whispers up at her.

She nods. 'I will be. I need to finish this.'

Flora turns around to face the hall. 'I'm not stupid. I've heard all the rumours. I'm a British spy because I'm Scottish. I'm a German spy because I speak German. The truth is I'm a pacifist. I'm on the side of peace and only peace. I don't agree with any kind of war. But I do believe in saving lives. I believe every life matters. Irish, British, and yes, German too.'

She turns back towards the stage. 'Mrs Reilly, as a dedicated churchgoer I'm sure you know that Jesus told us to love our neighbours as ourselves. Well, that includes Germans. Isn't that right, Father McRory?'

Flora looks at the priest directly. He seems uncomfortable and gives a nervous cough. 'In wartime these things can get complicated, Mrs Devine,' he says.

'It seems pretty simple to me,' Flora says. 'My daughter and son and the Lavelle children and Mamó Lavelle, they risked their lives

120

to save a young man who was burning alive. I'm very proud of what they did. We should all be proud. But no, we're in this hall talking about the poor boy murdering us in our sleep. He's someone's much-loved brother. Someone's much-loved son.' She stops for a second and takes a deep breath.

'Mr de Valera has managed to keep us out of this war,' she continues. 'Officially it's not a war, it's The Emergency. And we are lucky, so lucky. Our husbands and sons are here with us, at home in Blacksod, not fighting on some godforsaken battlefield in France, or yes, being blown up in a hospital tent like my poor brother, or crashing out of the sky and being burnt to a crisp like Hans. He barely has any hands left to murder anyone, they are so badly burned. Now I'm going home to give Hans morphine so he can get some rest. Anyone care to join me? Come and see if you're so interested. Look at his charred face and limbs and his poor broken body.'

She looks around the room. There's utter silence.

'I didn't think so. What are you all doing here? Go home and look after your loved ones. And hold them close. Thank your lucky stars we are not involved in this horrible, horrible war. Now, I have work to do.'

With that, Flora strides out of the hall. The door bangs behind her. It's so quiet in here you could hear a pin drop.

'Will we go too?' I whisper to Dad.

'No, stay here with me for a minute,' he says. 'It's not over yet.'

Miss Waldron stands up. 'She's right, this is nonsense. I completely support the poor German boy being looked after in the lighthouse until he's well enough to go to the Curragh. I'm with Mrs Devine.' She makes her way out too.

'I also agree with Mrs Devine,' Mr Lavelle says. 'The boy is no threat to anyone. My Ellen is nursing him, and she can attest to that. And I'm deeply proud of my mother and my children for their bravery. They are a credit to Blacksod, all of them.' He stands up and starts walking out of the hall.

Mamó stands up next. 'Shame on all of you,' she says. 'We're lucky to have a smart, educated lady like Mrs Devine in our community. Leave her be.' She walks out too, pulling a reluctant Sibby by the arm. Sibby's probably afraid she'll miss more drama.

Within minutes, the whole hall has cleared out after them, apart from the trio on the stage.

'Any questions for me, Father?' Dad says, sitting back in his chair and folding his arms across his chest. 'I've had to close the post office for the afternoon, so I'm all yours.'

Father McRory looks at Mrs Reilly and Mr Kennedy, and they both shake their heads. They look a bit shocked at Flora's words and the walk-out.

'I guess not,' Mrs Reilly says with a sniff. 'But I'm still not happy.'

'When were you ever happy, Olive?' Dad says under his breath.

I put my hand over my mouth to cover my smile. He's right, she always looks miserable.

Dad stands up. 'Then we'll be off. And I think you all owe my wife an apology, for wasting her time. She's a good woman, Flora, the best. Mrs Lavelle is right, we're lucky to have her in Blacksod. Come on, children, we're going home.' He leans down and says softly to me, 'Now, it's over, love.'

* * *

Walking out of the community hall, Dad says, 'Well, that was fun. They won't mess with Flora again lightly.'

'She really gave them what for.' Dannie punches his fists in the air, like he's shadow boxing. *'Pow, pow, pow!'*

Dad laughs. 'She really did. Grace, are you all right? You're very quiet.'

I shrug. For once I have nothing to say. Flora said everything and I could not be prouder of her. She was so strong and fierce that I'm completely overcome. Relieved, too – so relieved that my eyes start to well up.

'I thought Flora was in terrible trouble,' I admit. 'That Hans would be put in prison or something. I was really worried. She was amazing.'

'She really was,' Dad says. 'Ah, love, come here to me and don't be crying. All's well, and Hans will be fine.' He reaches over and gives me a hug. 'She's some woman, that wife of mine. And you're some daughter. I'm a lucky man. Now let's find Flora and get ourselves home. It's been a long day.'

Castellanus

With tops like castle turrets, these clouds can mean
unsettled weather is coming

CHAPTER 14

Sunday 14th May, 1944

Garda Collins arrives on the doorstep the following morning. I'm in the kitchen with Dad and the dogs. Flora and Dannie are checking the lighthouse bulb and cleaning the lens which magnifies its light so that you can see the beam shining strong and bright for miles and miles. All the windows around the lantern, inside and out, also need to be carefully rubbed down with vinegar and newspaper – it's a big job. If it's been stormy, the outside glass can become encrusted with salt from the seawater and it needs to be carefully cleaned off so the light can shine through it clearly.

Flora always rewards Dannie for his help with a couple of biscuits, but he'd do it anyway. Dannie loves the view from up there – you can see for miles, right across the bay to Achill Island. We sometimes sit up there and watch for dolphins with my binoculars. Flora doesn't mind as long as we take care going up and down the metal spiral staircase and we don't touch the lens with our grubby fingers. (That's aimed more at Dannie that me – it's remarkable how dirty my little brother's hands can get!)

Flora was quiet this morning and seemed tired, which isn't like her. I think yesterday took a lot out of her, even though she'd never admit it. Maybe, like me, she was worried about what would happen at the meeting. Sometimes I forget that grown-ups are just like us, with their own thoughts and feelings and worries.

Lucky and Poppy give Garda Collins their usual loud, barky greeting. When Dad welcomes him inside, he lets them both sniff his boots and trouser legs. Once they've calmed down, he gives each of them a rub behind the ears.

'They smell my dogs off me,' he says. He stands there for a moment, then says, 'Weather's breaking a bit.'

Dad nods. 'Aye, it is.'

Garda Collins takes off his hat and holds it in his hands.

'Cup of tea, Harold?' Dad asks him.

'I won't, thanks. Need to get back to the missus. I suppose you're wondering why I'm here. I'll come straight to the point. I had a phone call yesterday evening from the powers that be up at the Curragh. They have a military ambulance lined up to collect the German lad and bring him to the hospital at the internment camp. I know Flora's been keeping the doctor in Belmullet Hospital updated. I told them they'd have to wait until he's well enough to travel, and that it might be another week or so. Once Flora and the doctor are happy, you could let me know and they can send the military ambulance for him. If that's all right with you all, Tom?'

Dad smiles. 'Flora will be happy with that. Thanks. I appreciate you letting us know.'

Garda Collins twists his hat in his hands and stares down at it before looking up at Dad again. 'I heard about the meeting yesterday. The wife's sister was there. Told us the details. Sorry you got caught up in all that. I believe Flora made them all see sense.'

'She did,' Dad says.

'No better woman. How's he doing anyway? The German lad.'

'Still sleeping most of the time. But he's stable. Flora seems pleased enough with his progress.'

'Hans,' I tell Garda Collins. 'His name is Hans Holban.'

Dad gives me a bit of a look for interrupting but doesn't say anything.

'Aye, Hans,' Garda Collins says. 'Good girl yourself. I'm glad he's here with your family. I had a proper think and a talk with the missus. What Flora said about us being lucky to be out of the war, it hit home with her, pretty hard. Our three lads would have been called up by now if we lived in Britain. And if it was one of our sons in a plane crash, landing on enemy territory, we'd want him to be somewhere safe. With kind people. And we read the details of what you did for Hans in the paper, young Grace.' He looks at me, his brown eyes warm and kind. 'I had no idea you pulled him out of the flames like that. Took a lot of guts. How's your hand? I believe you got some burns and cuts.'

I look down at my hand. Flora checked my skin this morning, changed the dressings and gave me a fresh bandage. 'Much better today, thank you,' I tell him. 'Flora says the bandage can come off in a few days.'

'That's good to hear,' he says. 'You're your mother's daughter, all right. Brave little missy.'

'Thanks, Garda Collins,' I say, feeling warm inside. It's not often you hear grown-ups admit they were wrong. It's been quite a week!

Dad rubs my head. 'That she is. We're right proud of her.'

* * *

As I pick up the telephone receiver to ring in the 14:00 hours weather report, Garda Collins's words are still ringing in my ears. 'Brave little missy.' Thinking about it, I'm not so sure about the 'little missy' bit, but I liked being called brave.

After I've delivered the report, Maureen says, 'You sound more chipper today, Grace.'

'I guess I am. Despite the weather. It's just started raining again. Windy too. I think there's a squall on the way.'

'Hopefully it will clear up quickly. Cross all your fingers and toes, Grace. We could do with some fine weather soon.' She sounds a bit worried.

'How are you, Maureen?'

'Oh, I'm all right. Thanks for asking, Grace. Long hours and not much sleep, but this war can't go on forever.'

'Do you have any family in it? Fighting, I mean?'

The line goes quiet for a moment. Maybe I've been overfriendly or asked something I shouldn't have asked.

'I do,' she says softly. 'My fiancé, Reggie, is a pilot in the air corp. I'll tell you about him some day, but right now my supervisor is giving me the beady eye. Better run. *Slán*, Grace.'

'*Slán*, Maureen.'

As I put down the receiver I think about Maureen, sitting at her desk in the Met Office in Dunstable, worrying about her fiancé. Flora's right, we're lucky to be living in Ireland, well away from the war.

* * *

That evening the telephone rings in the office during dinner, and Flora goes to answer it. When she comes back, she has a strange expression on her face.

'It was Dunstable,' she says. 'They're looking for me to check all the instruments. Make sure they're all maintained and working correctly. At least I have the stupid anemometer fixed now. That thing is the bane of my life. Mentioned that they may need to increase the nightly reports soon and to stand by.'

Dad whistles. 'It's really stepping up. Did they say why?'

'No, but my guess is they're getting ready for some sort of sea or air operation. Something big. Obviously, this is top secret.' Flora presses her finger to her lips. 'Got it, Dannie?'

Dannie nods. 'Got it.'

'How long will the war go on, Flora?' I ask her. 'It has to end at some stage, right?'

She shrugs. 'We just don't know, pet. And until it does, the whole world is on hold, Ireland included. We just have to hang in there and try to live our lives regardless. And do what we can to help anyone who gets stuck here, like poor Hans. Speaking of which, I'd better go and check on him.'

'Ellen's in there reading to him,' I say. I popped my head in earlier to check if they needed anything. '*Grimms' Fairy Tales*,' I add.

'She's still here?' Flora looks at her wristwatch. 'She's very devoted. And that's rather sweet of her to find a German book to read him, even if it is in English.'

'That was my idea,' I say.

Flora smiles. 'You are a clever one, Grace.'

Fog

A blanket of water droplets that can
form over the land or sea

CHAPTER 15

Friday 19th May, 1944

In school, Sibby has truly sent me to Coventry and refuses to look at me, let alone talk to me. The other girls are taking her side and without anyone to chat to, the days crawl by. Sometimes I wish I was a boy. When they fight, they just thump each other and move on, but with girls it's a lot more complicated. And with Sibby, 'complicated' doesn't even start to cover it. I think she enjoys the drama of it all. Sometimes I catch her looking at me and then giving me the stink eye and tossing her head, making sure people see her. It's exhausting and I can't be bothered with it.

So instead of dealing with Sibby's theatrics all the way through lunch break, I sit inside and read. Miss Waldron checks on me from time to time, but largely she leaves me alone.

I'm reading my way through all the books on the shelves of the small school library at the back of the classroom. I started with *Great Expectations* by Charles Dickens. He tells a great story. It's full of mad characters, like on-the-run convicts and old ladies who wear crumbling lace wedding dresses. The language is a bit old-fashioned, but boy does he have some imagination!

Now I'm reading a big thick book about a scary white whale called *Moby Dick*. It's pretty old and the pages are yellow and smell a bit musty, but it keeps me busy. I can't bear to pick up my beloved *Anne of Green Gables* books at the moment as they remind me too much of Sibby.

At home, Hans is doing well. Flora borrowed a wheelchair from the hospital with a special wooden ledge sticking out the front to support his broken leg in its white plaster. On Thursday afternoon, she and Ellen lifted Hans into it and wheeled him down to the harbour to watch the fishing boats coming in. I hope he wasn't deafened by the seagulls squawking. They can get pretty loud when they smell dinner!

Hans still has bandages covering the worst of his burns, but he's awake a lot more now and Ellen says he's in less pain than he was. But I still hear him moan when she changes his dressings. He's able to say simple sentences in English now too – Ellen's a good teacher.

The military ambulance is booked for Friday of next week, the 26th of May. We're all going to miss him, but Ellen most of all. They've become the best of friends.

*** ***

The evening before Hans is being collected, Ellen wheels him into the kitchen, where I'm sitting finishing my homework. She places him opposite me and sits down on the chair beside me.

'Good evening, Grace,' Hans says in English. 'I must say you something.'

'*Tell* you something.' Ellen corrects him gently.

He smiles at her. '*Tell* you something. You save my life. I am always happy for this. Gateful. Very gateful. You brave. You kind. Ireland kind. Ellen kind.' He looks at Ellen and smiles again.

Ellen doesn't correct his English this time. She smiles back at him and for several seconds they just stare at each other, until Ellen breaks the gaze and looks at me instead.

'Hans would like you to take him for a walk,' she says. 'To say goodbye to the harbour and the lighthouse. He's quite taken with the lighthouse.' She presses her lips together. Her eyes are glittering, and I think she's trying not to cry.

'I'd love to,' I say. 'Are you coming too?'

'No, I'm going to stay here. Prepare his bandages. Make his bed for the last time. He'll be cold outside. I'll just get him some blankets.'

She fetches two blankets and puts one over Hans's legs and another around his shoulders. 'See you both in a while. Enjoy your walk.'

She blinks back tears as she turns and walks out of the kitchen. Poor Ellen, I think she's going to really miss Hans.

'Are you all right to push me?' Hans asks, switching back to German.

'You mean, am I strong enough?' I say in German. I grin at him. 'I pushed you out of that aeroplane, didn't I?'

He grins back. 'You did. But I meant your hand.'

'It's much better now. Look, no bandage.' I hold up my right hand. There's a plaster around my index finger where the deepest cut is, but other than that it's mostly healed up. 'So let's go!'

I grab the handles of the wheelchair and push him out the kitchen door, taking care on the low doorstep. We turn right, towards the harbour. The harbour road is a bit rocky, and I have to push extra hard when one of the wheels gets stuck in a pothole, but it's only a few yards from our kitchen door to the harbour and when we reach that surface it's hard stone, much easier to push the wheelchair across. I take Hans to the very end of the harbour wall and then stop, angling him so he's facing our lighthouse.

'Can we stay here for a few minutes?' he asks. 'I love this air.' He breathes in the salty air, then winces slightly. It must hurt his ribs to breathe in too deeply.

'Fishy and cold?' I say.

He laughs. 'Fresh and alive,' he says.

I sit on a bollard beside him and look down at the water. It's choppy today, gun-metal grey. The wind blows Hans's blond hair back off his face. The burns on his cheeks are starting to heal but his hands and legs are still covered in bandages, making him look like an Egyptian mummy.

'I will miss Blacksod,' he says. 'And I will miss you and Ellen very much. I have never met anyone like her. So clever. So kind and patient. I would like to write to her and keep in touch. Do you think she'd like me to?'

'Yes,' I say firmly. 'I think she'd love it.'

He nods, his eyes twinkling. 'Good,' he says. 'And thank you, Grace. For everything. I would not be here without you. I have no way of repaying you, but I promise I will never forget you. The Irish girl who saved my life.'

* * *

I'm not expecting to see Ellen on Friday after Hans has gone, but when I get home from school she's sitting in his wheelchair in the kitchen, her eyes closed.

'Ellen?'

She jumps, her movement sending the wheelchair skittling backwards a little on the kitchen tiles. She puts her hands on the wheels to stop it and climbs out. 'Sorry, I was miles away.' She wipes the corner of her eye with a knuckle. 'It's been such an intense two weeks and now Hans has gone, it all seems like a dream. Does that make sense?'

I nod. 'He's your friend. You spent a lot of time together. It's normal to miss him.'

She smiles at me. 'Exactly. He's promised to write, but I'm worried about what will happen to him. Will he be held 'til the end of the war? Or sent back to Germany to fight? And what's the prisoner of war camp like? Will he be looked after there? He's still not well.'

I don't have the answers to any of her questions, so I stay quiet and let her talk.

'Will you help me with the letters?' she says. 'Translate them for us so we can understand each other?'

''Course I will,' I say.

'Thanks. You have to promise you'll keep everything we say to each other to yourself, though. You can't tell Sibby or Mamó or Flora a thing. Especially Sibby.'

I shrug. 'She's not talking to me anyway.'

'Still? I'm sorry to hear that, but she'll come around. So you'll keep what's in the letters a secret?'

'Cross my heart and hope to die,' I say, crossing myself. 'Stick a needle in my eye.'

'Thanks.' She beams at me. 'You're a life saver.'

Reading secret letters between a handsome German airman and a beautiful Irish girl who helped nurse him back to health ... Is she kidding? It's like the plot of one of the swooney Hollywood matinees Sibby's always going on about! I beam back at Ellen. I almost say, 'I can't wait!' but I manage to stop myself.

'You're welcome,' I say instead. But roll on the first letter!

Roll cloud

An unusual long, tubular cloud.
They can be associated with storms

CHAPTER 16

Wednesday 31st May, 1944

The following Wednesday afternoon, after walking home from school with Dannie, I find Ellen sitting on the doorstep outside the lighthouse building.

'Hi, Grace.' She stands up and walks towards me, waving something in her hand. 'I got a letter!' From the radiant smile on her face, I know it's from Hans.

My heart lifts. It's the most exciting thing that's happened to me all day. School was boring, boring, boring. Sibby's still doing her stupid Coventry thing. I haven't talked to anyone since breakfast apart from Dannie and Miss Waldron, and they don't really count.

I look around for our car, but it's not there. Flora must be in Belmullet on an errand.

The dogs hear us and start barking. 'Dannie, you go on inside. The dogs are waiting for you. I'll come in and help you with your homework soon. Actually, would you like to take them for a walk first? Liam might go with you. You can take some biscuits with you.'

He tilts his head. 'Are you trying to get rid of me or something?'

'Yes,' I say. 'We have girls' stuff to talk about. Unless you want to hear all about the boys we like.' I make a kissing sound and he backs away from me.

'Yuck! Disgusting!' He pushes past Ellen and goes inside.

Ellen laughs. 'That worked a treat.'

Seconds later, Dannie's back outside and running past us with the dogs.

It's a grey day and there's drizzle in the air. It's not nice enough to sit outside, so we sit down at the kitchen table instead.

'Would you like some tea?' I ask Ellen.

'Not at all. I'm dying to know what this says. I can make out a few words but that's all.' She pulls the letter out of the envelope and hands it to me. Her eyes are sparkling.

It looks like a boy's writing to me. It's neat, the letters clearly formed and quite square, almost blocky. Hans's hands are too damaged to hold a pen.

'Who wrote it for him?' I ask. 'Do you know?'

Ellen shakes her head. 'He must have dictated it to another German airman or something. So it's unlikely to have anything too personal in it.'

I wiggle my eyebrows at her. 'So I shouldn't expect any mushy bits or romantic poems then?'

'Grace! It's not like that, we're just friends.' But her eyes are sparkling again, and her cheeks are a bit rosy.

I smile and wiggle my eyebrows again. 'For now.'

She gives a laugh. 'Just read the letter, Grace.'

I start reading out loud.

> Military Hospital
> Internment Camp – G Camp
> The Curragh
> Co Kildare
> Friday 26th May, 1944

Dear Ellen,

I have arrived safely at the Curragh. The journey was long and a bit bumpy, but I survived. There were two Irish soldiers travelling with me and also a kind nurse called Sheila who works at the hospital and is engaged to one of the doctors. She speaks a bit of German too, which is helpful.

I was brought to the Military Hospital in the internment camp. There are two areas in the prisoner of war camp, one for the Allies called B Camp and one for the Germans called G Camp.

I can't believe they put the Allied soldiers and the German soldiers so close together – sworn enemies. But they have!

As soon as I arrived at the hospital a German officer visited me, Kapitänleutnant Joachim Quedenfeld. He told me I would be treated well and that he'd visit me daily to check on me and would help me transcribe letters for you.

He even left two German novels on my bedside table. I've already started *Renni the Rescuer: A Dog of the Battlefield* and it's pretty good.

Ellen, they have all been so nice to me here. I cannot tell you how relieved I am. The hospital is quite basic – it's a large metal hut – but it's clean and tidy and I feel safe here.

I hear Ellen make a noise, an 'Oh' and then a happy sigh. I look over at her. She's blinking back a few tears.

'What a relief!' she says, wiping her eyes with her fingers. 'I was imagining all kinds of things, mud and rats and I don't know what. But it sounds like he's being well looked after. And they're kind. That's the best news of all! They're kind. Phew.' She blows out her breath in a whoosh.

'It is good news,' I say. 'Will I keep going?'

'Oh, yes! Yes, please. Sorry to interrupt.'

I continue reading.

Ellen, I feel so blessed right now. To be alive. To be somewhere safe. To have met you. For your nursing and your time and your friendship.

Please tell Flora and Tom how grateful I am to them for taking me in. And to Dannie for lending me his room. To Grace for being my translator and for saving my life. I owe her everything.

I will never forget their kindness. And my best wishes to Poppy and Lucky. Especially Poppy. The one who found me.

I will go now, Ellen, as I cannot keep Joachim any longer. Sheila says she will post this for me in the morning. I've told her about you as best I can. She says to say hello.

I will write again soon.

Your friend,

Hans XXX

Ellen is beaming from ear to ear. 'What a lovely letter,' she says.

'Are you going to write back to him?' I say.

She grins. 'I thought you'd never ask.'

Ellen's letter is short and simple, telling him how relieved she is that he's being well taken care of and how she hopes to visit him one day when he's better.

I look at her. 'Is that it?'

'What do you mean?'

'It's very factual. Are you not going to say how much you miss him?'

Her cheeks go a bit pink again. 'Do you think I should?'

'Yes! The poor man is lying in his hospital bed thinking about you. Telling all the nurses about you. Well, one nurse anyway. You should definitely tell him you miss him.'

'OK, then, you can put that in. Say something like … "I hope you continue to get better and I miss talking to you".'

I hope you continue to get better so I can visit you really soon if that's allowed (will you ask?). And I miss you so much. I think about you all the time. You're an amazing person, Hans. I've never met anyone like you before. Stay strong. We will be together again soon.

I'm quite pleased with how it sounds. And it's almost what Ellen said to write. Kind of.

Ellen points at the German phrase for 'amazing person' – *unglaublicher Mensch*. 'What have you written there?'

'Strong person.'

Her eyes narrow. 'Are you sure?'

I shrug. 'Sometimes the words in German are longer than in English. What will I put at the end? "Love, Ellen"?'

'No! Not "love". How did he close his letter?'

'"Your friend, Hans" and then three kisses,' I tell her.

'Use the same. "Your friend, Ellen".'

'And three kisses?'

'Go on then. But only three.'

I smile and do as she says.

'I'm going to drop it up to the post office now,' she says. 'Thanks for your help, Grace. You're a star.'

'Any time,' I say. 'As long as you invite me to the wedding.' I start singing, 'Daisy, Daisy, give me your answer do …'

'Grace!' She squeals and thumps my arm.

I just laugh and wiggle my eyebrows at her again, making her laugh.

'You're funny, Grace Devine. And I'm off to the post office before you say anything else nutty.'

As she leaves, I dance around the kitchen singing the rest of the song. 'I'm half crazy, all for the love of you. It won't be a stylish marriage, I can't afford a carriage ...'

Pyrocumulus

Clouds that form over great heats, like forest fires
or volcanoes. They are one of the few clouds created
by humans, along with contrails

CHAPTER 17

Wednesday 31st May & Thursday 1st June, 1944

'Blacksod 003. Grace speaking. How can I help you?'

'Grace, it's Maureen. Is Flora there?'

'No, she's in Belmullet, I think. She's been gone a while. She should be back soon enough. Can I take a message?'

'Yes, please do. It's important.' Maureen sounds a bit flustered. 'Can you make sure to tell her as soon as she's in the door? Have you got a pencil and a piece of paper?'

'Yes, all set.'

'Right, here goes. We need hourly weather reports starting right now. Day *and* night.'

'Woah! That's a lot of weather reports.'

'But you'll do it, right?'

'Of course. It's our job.'

'Good woman,' she says. 'Every hour during the night, yes? And you've written the message down for Flora?'

I'm hardly going to forget that news, but I write it down anyway. 'Yes! For how long? A few days? A week?'

'That's a good question, Grace. One I can't answer, I'm afraid, or talk about. But it's vitally important that the figures are as accurate as you can make them. Especially the air pressure. You need to check each reading carefully. Have you got all that?'

'Yes. I'm sure Flora will be back for the next weather report, and if she's not, I'll do it.'

'Thank you. And Grace, no-one ever says this to you or to Flora, but your work is important. *Really* important. You are appreciated more than you could ever know. By me and by everyone here.'

'Thanks, Maureen. That's really nice of you. I hope they appreciate your work too. In Dunstable and in Portsmouth.'

The line goes quiet for a moment. Oops, maybe I shouldn't have said 'Portsmouth'.

'It's been …' she pauses for a second and then adds, 'interesting. The next few days are going to be busy for both of us. Once day I hope we can talk more, get to know each other properly. Until later, Grace. *Slán.*'

'*Slán*, Maureen.'

A weather report every hour the whole way through the night, for days and maybe even weeks. That's going to be a challenge!

* * *

During dinner, Flora makes a rota for the new weather reporting. 'We have to take this very seriously,' she says. 'Grace, are you all right to do some of the night shift?'

I nod. 'Yes.'

'I want to help with the night shift too,' Dannie says.

Dad gives Flora a stern look, but she ignores him. 'That's very helpful of you, Dannie,' she says. 'I'll do the 10pm to 1am shift. Tom, if you could take the 2am and 3am shifts so I can get some sleep. Grace and Dannie, you'll cover the 4am to 6am shifts. Then I'll be back again at 7am.'

'The children can't get up at four in the morning, Flora,' Dad says. 'Are you mad? What about school? They'll be exhausted.'

'They'll be fine,' Flora says. 'They're young, they don't need as much sleep as we do. It will only be for a few days.'

'You don't know that,' he says. 'It could go on for weeks.'

'And if it does, we'll manage. Tom, listen to me.' She puts her hand on one of his. 'I've said it before. Something important is planned, something that could change the direction of the whole war. I've been going over and over it in my head and I think I know what's going to happen.' She takes a deep breath. 'The Allies are getting ready to invade France. And the sooner the fighting ends, the better, for everyone. We can't stay up all night, just the two of us. We need to get the weather reports spot on. We can't slip up. And you have the post office to run on top of that and I have all the weather instruments and the light to check. To do that, we both need to get some sleep. We need the children's help. Let them help us, Tom. Please. They're well able.'

Flora looks so serious. I wonder if she's correct about the invasion?

Dad nods. 'You're right. We'd be glad of your help, Grace and Dannie. Let's do this together, as a family.'

* * *

Early hours of Thursday 1st June, 1944

I thought I'd have to shake Dannie awake before our shift, but he's standing at the end of my bed, fully dressed, at quarter to four in the morning, just as my alarm clock rings. He's back in his own room now that Hans has gone. Poppy and Lucky have joined him, and they bark a little at the tinny alarm clock bells.

'Shush, you two!' I mutter. There's a bit of light coming in from the open door into the hall.

I groan, roll over and slap at the top of the clock to turn it off. 'Is it that time already?'

'I set mine a bit early,' Dannie says. 'Wasn't that clever?'

I groan again. I really don't like early mornings. 'Suppose so. Give me a few minutes. I'm barely awake. And bring those two outside for a run around and a wee.'

'Will do,' he says, sounding annoyingly chipper. The sun isn't up yet so I switch on my bedside lamp and pull my clothes on, still feeling groggy.

I walk outside to find Dannie. It's dark and the cold air jolts me more awake. I see a flickering light. He already has the Stevenson screen open and is reading the thermometer. He's wearing Flora's head torch so he can see. I'm impressed. He's a lot more organised that I thought he'd be.

'Have you got your notebook on you?' I ask him.

He nods. 'Yes. I'll write down the temperature and the rain readings carefully.'

'Good. I'll meet you in the office.' I have a good look up at the sky. There's no sign of the moon or stars with the heavy cloud cover. As I stand there it starts to drizzle. I walk quickly inside.

In the office I check all the instruments and jot down their readings in the ledger. The air pressure is still low and has dropped since Flora's 3am reading. When Dannie comes in, I add his readings to the weather ledger.

At 4am on the dot, I ring Dunstable.

'Dunstable 2100. How may I help you?'

'Maureen, it's Grace. I wasn't expecting you to be manning the telephone. Do you ever sleep?'

'Not much these days. I grab naps between the reports. Needs must. How's things in Blacksod?'

'Drizzling outside. Heavy cloud cover. But here's the official 04:00 hours report.

Barometer 12.4 falling quickly -12

Wind direction SW

Wind speed 2 knots …'

I give her the full report.

'Thanks, Grace. I'll pass this on immediately to Mr Stagg. I mean … to my superiors.'

'Did you just say Mr Stagg? The weather man from Scotland?'

'You know him?' Maureen sounds very surprised.

'He visited the lighthouse a few years ago. He had tea with us.'

'Did he now? How extraordinary. Have to run, Grace. Are you on duty at five?'

'Yes and at six.'

'Talk to you then. *Slán*.'

'*Slán*, Maureen.'

'Is that it?' Dannie asks me as soon as I've put down the receiver. 'Can we go back to bed now?'

'If you like. I don't feel very sleepy now, so I think I'll read. But you sleep if you want to. I'll wake you up before five.'

I'm reading my birthday book, *Swallows and Amazons*, about

some friends who have adventures during their summer holidays. There are boats and pirates and a mystery, and it's great fun. I'm dying to get back to it.

'There isn't much time to sleep,' he says, 'so maybe I'll draw.'

We settle ourselves in the kitchen, Dannie at the table with his pencils and sketchpad and me in the armchair beside the range with my book, the dogs on their blankets by my feet. It's all surprisingly calm. But then I remember one of Flora's weather sayings, 'the calm before the storm', and feel a little uneasy.

Kelvin-Helmholtz

One of the most unusual clouds in the world,
it looks like waves breaking over the shore

CHAPTER 18

Saturday 3rd June, 1944

On Saturday morning, my alarm clock goes off at quarter to four. No Dannie or the dogs at the end of my bed this morning. I drag myself up. I feel more tired than I did the past two mornings. I tried to go to bed earlier than usual last night, but I couldn't fall asleep. I think the lack of sleep is starting to catch up with me. I yawn so deeply that my jaw cracks. It must be wild outside – I can hear the roar of the wind and the smack of rain hitting the windowpanes.

Yesterday, I almost fell asleep in school. Miss Waldron asked me to go outside to collect some oak leaves as we were doing photosynthesis in science. The fresh air woke me up a bit, but it was hard to stay alert and by lunchtime I was flagging. I came home and had a nap before helping Flora with the anemometer, which was rattling yet again. She's right, that thing really is a curse! Flora says it's because we get such strong winds at Blacksod. They're not designed for Atlantic strength storms, she reckons.

I drag myself out of bed and start to get dressed. There's a nip in the air so I pull my thick jumper over my shirt, put my heavy green overalls on top and go to wake Dannie. He's snoring gently when I shake his arm.

'Dannie,' I say quietly. 'Time to get up.'

'What? Already?'

'Yes. You must have turned your alarm off and dozed off again.'

I switch on his bedside lamp. 'I'll meet you outside. Be quick now.'

When I open the kitchen door with the dogs behind me, they don't run straight out like they normally do. I don't blame them – it's revolting out there. Lashing rain and windy too. No moon again, and heavy cloud cover. Dannie appears beside me.

'Yuck!' he says, looking out the doorway.

'You'll need your raincoat,' I tell him. 'I'll meet you in the office in a few minutes.' I'm expecting him to grumble and refuse to go outside, but to my surprise he doesn't.

'And my welly boots,' he says and goes off to find them.

As soon as I get into the office, I check the instruments. At seven knots, the wind speed is definitely stronger than yesterday or the day before. I check Dad's 03:00 hours report: five knots. At 02:00 hours, it was four knots. At 01:00 hours, two knots. It's getting windier and windier.

I check the barometer next. The reading now is exactly the same as it was at 03:00, 02:00 and 01:00 hours, according to the ledger: 19.2. That's strange. It's rarely exactly the same as the previous report unless it's very fine, stable weather. Flora told me that.

I read over all the figures from the previous three weather reports in the weather ledger. Nothing else is exactly the same – all the readings fluctuate, even just a little.

I peer at the barometer. It's a coiled metal instrument attached to a needle which makes a mark on graph paper fixed to a small drum. The needle mark on the graph paper is in exactly the same place as it has been since 01:00 hours.

Dannie runs in and gives me the readings from the rain gauge and the thermometers. The rainfall is well up on the readings from

153

earlier, and the temperature has dropped.

It's two minutes after four. Broken barometer or no broken barometer, I have to ring Maureen.

'Dunstable 2100. How can I help you?'

'Maureen, I'm going to give you all the figures now. But there's something up with the barometer. The weather is getting really bad over here. It's lashing rain, the wind's increasing and the temperature's dropping. Everything's signalling a storm is on the way.'

I can hear Maureen mutter 'Damn it' under her breath.

I keep going. 'But the barometer's been showing exactly the same pressure since 01:00 hours. That's not right, is it?'

'No. From what you're saying, the pressure should be dropping. I'm sorry, but I think you need to wake Flora. Get her to look at the barometer. Give me all the other readings and then ring me back when she's checked it. It's important, Grace. Speed is of the essence. Tell Flora we really, really need that barometer to be working right now.'

'Will do.'

Seconds later, I'm in Flora and Dad's room, shaking her arm, just like I did to Dannie's a little while ago.

She opens her eyes immediately. 'What's wrong?'

'It's the barometer. You need to check it. Maureen said it's urgent.'

'OK, give me a minute to throw on a jumper and I'll meet you in the office.'

Dad doesn't stir. He'd sleep through anything.

I go back into the office and a minute later, Flora joins me. She goes straight over to the barometer and studies the graph paper and then the needle and the coiled unit. 'You're right. It's not working.

The needle's stuck. Well done for spotting it. I'm going to have to take it apart and see what the problem is. It's going to take a while. Wish we had a back-up barometer, but we don't.'

Something occurs to me. 'The Lavelles do. A scientific one from Glasgow. Sibby told me about it.'

'Really? It's very early, but do you think they'd let you take a reading? Just until this one's back in action.'

I look at the clock on the wall. It's only ten past four. Plus Sibby's not even speaking to me.

Flora takes my silence as a no. She sighs. 'I'll ring Maureen and tell her I'll do my best to get this one back in service for the 05:00 hours report. She might be better getting a pressure reading from another weather station until then.'

But I heard the urgency in Maureen's voice. The reading is important – vitally important. And readings from the other weather stations aren't as useful as our reading, Flora said so. We are the weather station that the Atlantic weather hits first.

I take a deep breath. 'Wait! I'll ask Sibby. And if she won't do it, I'll ask Mamó. She'll understand if I explain it's urgent. And I'll make sure to say it's top secret.'

* * *

I'm standing on the Lavelles' doorstep, my heart racing. It's so early. I hope I don't give Mamó a heart attack! Even though she seems sturdy, she is pretty old. I can't worry about that now. I bang on the door, hard.

A light goes on in the upstairs bedroom to the right, Mamó's room. I've been in the house so many times I know it like my own. Seconds later a light goes on in the hall and the front door swings open. Mamó stands there with a man's checked dressing gown pulled over her nightie. There's a cotton mobcap on her head. She looks alarmed when she sees me.

'Grace. Are you all right? It's cats and dogs out there. Come on inside.' She closes the hall door behind me, shutting out the rain and wind.

'I need Sibby's help,' I say in a low voice. I don't want to wake the whole household. Water drips from my raincoat onto the hall tiles. 'Our barometer is on the blink, and we need to take an urgent air pressure reading for the weather report at five.'

'You do them at night?'

'Every hour at the moment.'

She gives a whistle. 'I'll wake her up. I'm sure she'll be happy to help. Weather obsessed, that girl. She's set up all kinds of rain pots and things in the back garden. You and your mam got her into it.'

I'm surprised. Sibby never said anything to me about setting up her own weather station.

'Thanks, Mamó. Just to warn you, she might not be all that pleased to see me. She's not exactly talking to me right now.'

Mamó goes quiet for a moment and looks at me. 'How long has this been going on?'

I shrug. 'A while.'

'More than a few days?'

I nod silently, staring down at the red and black floor tiles. I don't want to land Sibby in trouble but I can't lie, not to Mamó.

Her eyes go soft. 'I'm disappointed in her. That's unkind,

whatever you've done. Has she the other girls following her?'

I nod again.

'Ah you poor creature, is anyone at school talking to you?'

I feel a wave of sadness and I swallow, willing myself not to cry. 'Not really,' I say in a whisper.

She shakes her head and makes a few tut-tutting noises. 'Ah, Sibby.'

'Please don't say anything,' I say. 'She'll know I told you and it will make things worse.'

She looks at me again, her eyes soft, and then gives a gentle smile. 'Are you sure, my love?'

'Positive.'

'As you wish. I'll go up and get her now.'

As she goes upstairs, I look down the hall towards the door to Mr Lavelle's study, wondering where exactly the barometer is. I'm about to peek inside the door when Sibby appears at the top of the stairs. It's hard to make out her expression as she walks down, a jumper pulled over a flannel nightie with pink kittens on it. I recognise it from sleepovers when we were little.

'Nice nightie,' I say. 'Very grown up.'

'Are you crazy?' she hisses, ignoring my nightie comment. 'It's half four in the morning.'

My heart lifts. At least she's talking to me!

'It's an emergency,' I say. 'I need a reading from your barometer. Ours is acting up. The needle's stuck. Flora's trying to fix it now.'

Her eyebrows shoot up. 'What kind of emergency? Who needs a weather report before the sun comes up? Spill the beans or I'm not helping you.'

I take a deep breath. Here goes! 'Every hour we send a weather report to the Met Office in Dunstable, near London. And they send it on to the war office in Portsmouth.'

Her eyes light up. That's got her attention! 'Go on,' she says.

'They use it to help plot things like operations. And invasions. Flora thinks the Allies are about to invade France. They need to know if there's a storm on the way. If there is, the air pressure will be dropping rapidly. They can't invade by sea or air during a storm. It would be too dangerous.'

Sibby's eyes are now as big as the moon. 'An invasion? How exciting!'

'Sibby! Loads of soldiers are going to get killed.'

'It's still exciting. I can give you ground temperature and rainfall too, if you like. I've set up my own miniature weather station in the garden.'

'Mamó said. You never told me about that.'

'You're not the only smart one around here, you know. Drama is my first love, naturally, but I'm pretty interested in the weather too. If you weren't so rubbish at listening, you might know that.'

What is she talking about? I'm great at listening! I want to jump in and argue with her, tell her she's being ridiculous, but I stop myself. I think for a second. Hang on, what if she's right? Maybe I am rubbish at listening. Then I remember what Miss Waldron said about friendship and saying sorry.

'I'm sorry,' I say. 'I'll try harder to listen to you.'

Sibby seems very surprised by my apology. We stand there staring at each other for a few seconds. It's really awkward, and I can feel my cheeks pinking up.

'And I'm sorry too,' she says eventually. 'I know you didn't mean to leave me out of the article. I was upset. It was mean of me to send you to Coventry.'

'That's OK,' I say. 'I got a lot of reading done at breaktime and lunch.'

She laughs and nods down the hall. 'Come on, bookworm, let's get you that barometer reading.'

'So you're going to help me? Does that mean we're friends again?'

She shrugs. 'I guess. School is boring without you. Maria is a prize ninny. If she gives me any more stupid beauty tips, I'll scream.'

'School is so boring without *you*,' I say. I take a deep breath. 'And I really am sorry about the article. I was so nervous I didn't say much. I was too scared. Flora said I wasn't to mention Hans being at our house and I was paranoid about letting it slip. The journalist should have interviewed you. You'd have been much better.'

'I would,' she says. 'I was made for press interviews, I'm a natural.'

I smile at her. I love Sibby. Confident, bonkers and so much fun!

'I'll never leave you out again,' I say. 'Of anything. Pinkie promise.' I hold out my little finger.

She grips it with her little finger. 'Pinkie promise. Now let's get that reading and help keep the invasion safe. You know what this means, don't you?'

'What?' I ask.

'I was right,' she says smugly. 'About Flora. She's an Allied weather spy. You are too. The weather girls. Sounds like a blockbuster matinee to me!' Her eyes twinkle and she frames her head with her hands. 'Starring Elizabeth Lavelle as the girl who saves the day.'

I hadn't thought about it that way. 'I guess we are weather spies. But you have to keep it top secret, Sibby. Swear to me.'

She crosses herself dramatically. 'Cross my heart and hope to die. Stick a needle in my eye.' Sibby loves nothing better than a good secret. And this secret is so big I'm sure she'll keep it! 'Let's go, Billy O!' she says, grabbing my arm. 'Time to save those sailors.'

'Sibby! Shush!'

She just laughs.

Arcus

A long, dark cloud which moves along a
storm's front edge

CHAPTER 19

Saturday 3rd June, 1944

I run back home through the driving rain and ring Maureen with the barometer reading from Sibby's house.

'Dunstable 2100. How can I help you?'

'Maureen, we have an accurate barometer reading for you now.'

'Thank goodness. Well done! Now, be quick, I have James on the other line, champing at the bit for the report.'

'Will do.

Barometer 12.7 falling rapidly -18

Wind direction SW ...'

Maureen interrupts me. 'Go back to the barometer, please. Did you say 12.7?'

'Yes, 12.7.'

'And the last reading you have before that is 19.2?'

'That's right.'

'And you're sure about that?'

'Yes. Positive.'

She swears under her breath. 'All right then, continue.'

I give her the rest of the report, including the cloud cover, which is getting heavier and heavier.

'Thank you, Grace,' she says when I've finished. 'Can you hold there for a moment?' The line goes quiet, and I can hear Maureen talking to someone on another line. Then she's back.

'Mr Stagg would like you to double check the wind direction and the barometer reading. Can you do that?'

'Flora is taking apart our barometer right now. It's in bits on the kitchen table. There's a proper scientific one in our neighbour's house – that's where I took the latest reading from – but it will take me a few minutes to get there and home again. Can I ring you back?'

'Yes, yes. Quick as you can.'

* * *

And so it goes, all day Saturday from five in the morning. Backwards and forwards to Sibby's house for barometer readings every hour. It's a pain that Sibby doesn't have a telephone, but very few houses in Blacksod do. We can't move the Lavelles' barometer either, as it takes a while for barometers to settle after being shifted and the readings wouldn't be accurate. At least it's Saturday and there's no school.

The air pressure is plunging, and by lunchtime the wind is almost at gale force. When I ring Maureen at 1pm and give her the 13:00 hours report, she sounds like I've told her someone has died.

'Lordy,' she says. 'From the wind direction, the storm's going to hit England and then France. That's terrible news.'

'I wouldn't like to be on the water,' I say. 'The sea is so choppy. And the rain is coming down something terrible.' I'm getting soaked running the short distance between my house and Sibby's house, even with my raincoat and wellies on.

'I'd better get a shift on, Grace. Talk to you again at two. *Slán*.'

'*Slán*, Maureen.'

* * *

Flora still hasn't got the barometer working by Saturday evening.

'Will you go and check that the Lavelles are happy for us to invade their house tonight to use their barometer?' she asks. 'We'll need to do them all ourselves, even if Sibby or Mamó offer. We need to stand by our figures and make sure they are accurate.'

I'm not sure she's realises what she's just said – 'invade'. But then she does.

'Oops, "invade".' She shakes her head. 'A Freudian slip, that's what they call it. When you're thinking of something, and it comes out in your word choice. I've been praying for the Allied soldiers and sailors. They must be sitting on ships right now, waiting for their orders.'

Her eyes fill with tears, and she wipes them away. 'Sorry, Grace. It's been such an intense day. And all the phone calls and the war stuff make me think of Alfie. Dear old Alfie.' Her eyes fill up again and she presses her lips together. She nods down at the barometer, which is still in pieces on the kitchen table. 'Rain or no rain, I need a break from this. I'm heading outside for a walk.'

'I'll run down to the Lavelles' and ask them about the barometer,' I say.

'Thanks, pet.'

* * *

Mamó welcomes me inside and brings me down to the kitchen where Sibby is sitting at the table.

'We're happy to help,' Mamó says, when I ask her about taking barometer readings every hour until Flora has ours fixed. 'We all have to do our bit for the war effort. Get those poor boys home as soon as possible.'

I explain that Flora or I will do the daytime checks, then Flora will do 10pm to 1am and Dad will do 2am and 3am. I don't use the twenty-four-hour clock system we use for the weather reports, as I don't want to confuse her.

'I'm on duty from 4am to 6am,' I say.

'I can run the readings up to you if you like,' Sibby offers.

'Flora says we need to do them ourselves in case someone in the Met Office asks, but thanks for the offer,' I say.

'I'll get up and help you then,' she says. 'Keep you awake.'

'Are you sure?'

'What are friends for?' She smiles and brushes her hair back off her face. 'Besides, it might make me famous one day.'

I don't like to tell her that she's gone bonkers. All the war stuff is top secret, and by the time it's not classified anymore – years and years from now – honestly, who would be interested in two girls doing weather reports in a tiny Irish village? But I say nothing. Sibby is talking to me again. Sibby is calling me her friend. That's enough for me!

Mamma

A storm cloud that has strange pouches or bulges hanging
from the base. Also known as mammatus

CHAPTER 20

Sunday 4th June, 1944

At half three on Sunday morning my alarm dings, waking me. I'm groggy at first – it feels like I've only been asleep for a few minutes. My sheets and blankets are in a muddle from all my tossing and turning. There's been an almighty storm raging all night and I could hear the wind howling and the rain battering my window, keeping me awake.

My mind also kept me awake. I couldn't stop thinking about what Flora said about the Allied troops sitting on ships, waiting to sail to France to invade. At least I hope they are waiting and not trying to sail in this terrible weather.

I drag on my clothes and stagger through the rain over to Sibby's house. When I knock gently on the door, it opens immediately and there she is, grinning at me.

'Why are you smiling?' I ask her. 'I'm soaked and tired and it's horrible o'clock in the morning.'

'We're changing history, Grace. I've decided to write a play about it. I'll star as myself, naturally.'

I roll my eyes at her, but I can't help myself – I have to grin back. 'Sibby, let's just concentrate on our job, OK? The weather report.'

* * *

The storm rages all morning as we go back and forth to Sibby's house, while Flora tries to get our barometer to work. She's making progress, but there are still tools and bits of metal and solder all over the kitchen table, so we have to eat with our plates on our knees instead. But no one minds.

Breakfast is quiet. We're all exhausted from the hourly reports and the lack of sleep.

'How long will we be doing the weather stuff for?' Dannie asks with a yawn, sending his plate skittering on his knee. A piece of sausage falls to the floor and Poppy wolfs it down. Dad made us sausage sandwiches as a treat. 'Will we be going to school on Monday?' he asks.

Flora shrugs. 'I have no idea. But my gut feeling is that once this storm passes, things may change pretty quickly. We'll just have to wait and see.'

* * *

At half past eleven, Sibby flings open our kitchen door and runs inside. Her cheeks are bright red and her breath is huffy, like she's sprinted the whole way to our house. I'm sitting at the kitchen table watching Flora work on the barometer. She found the fault, which was in the needle mechanism, and has just managed to fix it with a new needle mechanism she made with the help of her soldering iron. We both look up at Sibby.

'It's changing!' Sibby says. 'The air pressure's changing. It's way up to 97. I thought you'd want to know.'

'Are you sure?' Flora asks.

Sibby nods. 'I've been watching the needle carefully. I'm sure.'

'Let's go and see,' Flora says.

We grab our coats and follow. We run behind Sibby, rush in the Lavelles' front door and go straight into the office. Flora stares at the barometer's needle. Sibby's right, the needle on the graph paper has stopped falling and is now lifting. As we watch, it lifts upwards another fraction.

'Girls,' Flora says, 'I think the storm's blowing through. We need to ring Dunstable immediately. This could change everything.'

Incus

An incus is part of a cumulonimbus storm cloud and
looks like a huge canopy of cloud stretching out over
miles. It sometimes has the shape of a blacksmith's anvil
('incus' is the Latin word for anvil)

CHAPTER 21

Tuesday 6th June, 1944

On Tuesday morning, the phone rings at ten to eight. Flora's already outside checking the anemometer. Miraculously it survived the storm, which, as predicted, has blown through. The weather is a lot better today – the sun's even shining for the first time in days.

I'm at the kitchen table with Dad and Dannie, who are both tucking into sausage sandwiches again. It's become a bit of a habit over the last few days. The telephone rings.

'I'll get it,' I say. I jump up and run into the office. 'Blacksod 003,' I answer.

'Grace, it's Maureen.'

'Do you need the weather forecast early?'

'Not at all. You can give it to us at nine today, in fact. We don't need one until then. And you deserve a break. Switch on your radio to the BBC, quick! It's important. There'll be an announcement at eight o'clock on the button. I'll ring you back straight after and explain everything, I promise.' The line goes dead.

I go back into the kitchen and tell them what Maureen said. Dannie goes out to the garden to call Flora inside, and Dad crouches down beside the radio, tuning it in. Dannie comes back in and sits beside Poppy, hugging his arms around her neck.

Flora rushes in and flops down on the armchair in front of the stove. 'They're announcing the invasion,' she says.

'How do you know?' I ask.

She shrugs. 'Stands to reason, all the commotion of the last few days and nights.'

'Let's see if you're right, Flora,' Dad says. He's tuned in the radio now; he turns it up and sits on the arm of Flora's chair. We all stare at the radio, waiting.

There's classical music for a few minutes – piano – and then a clipped English voice says, 'It's eight o'clock. 'This is a special bulletin read by John Snagge. D-Day has come.'

I gasp out loud. Flora was right! I listen, gripped.

Flora reaches out for Dad's hand and squeezes it. Dannie's eyes are glued to the radio, his mouth open.

'Early this morning the Allies began the assault of the north-western face of Hitler's European fortress. Under the command of General Eisenhower, Allied naval forces, supported by strong air forces, began landing Allied armies on the northern coast of France. I will be back at half past eight with more information.'

The classical music comes back on, and Dad gives a long whistle. 'You were right, Flora. The Allies have bloody well invaded. No wonder they needed so many weather reports. We helped make sure they didn't set off for France in the middle of a storm.'

'What happens now?' Dannie asks.

'We wait,' Dad says.

'And we hope this invasion will bring an end to the war,' Flora adds. 'Those poor boys and men on both sides. What they must be going through right now. War is brutal.' There are tears in Flora's eyes. She sits up a bit. 'Let's take the dogs for a walk, Tom. Dannie, Grace, will you come with us? We can go up the hill. I for one

172

could do with some fresh air.'

The phone rings again. 'That'll be Maureen,' I say. 'She promised she'd ring us back and explain a bit more about what's happening. Would you like to take it, Flora?'

Flora looks at me for a second, then smiles. 'No. You take it, Grace. We'll wait for you.'

I run into the office and whip up the receiver. 'Maureen, is that you?'

'It is indeed.'

'So that's what all the weather reports were about, the D-Day invasion?'

'Yes. I'm sorry I couldn't tell you much, it was top secret. But what I can tell you is that your weather reports stalled the invasion. Without them, our troops might have been caught up in that terrible storm. Because of you, they waited until the storm passed. Not that you can tell anyone about it, of course. But I thought you'd like to know. Between friends.'

'Thanks, Maureen. My lips are sealed. What happens now? Do you still need so many weather reports?'

'No. It will go back to the usual schedule now. I'll fill Flora in later. And all the extra telephone calls won't be necessary.'

'Oh,' I say. 'I see.' My voice sounds flat even to my ears. I'll miss talking to Maureen. And I know it's a war and all very serious and everything, but Sibby is right, it is exciting knowing top-secret things that other people don't know. Being 'weather spies', as she calls it.

'You sound tired,' Maureen says. 'You'll be able to get a lot more sleep now.'

'But what about you, Maureen? You must be exhausted. Is Reggie involved in D-Day?' I hold my breath waiting for her reply. Maybe I shouldn't have asked.

'Yes, but don't worry, he's safe. Today anyway.'

'That's great news. I'm off to walk the dogs now with my family, so I'll say goodbye for now. I'll talk to you again at the next weather report.'

'Yes, indeed. I know the last few nights have been a bit intense. You did an amazing job. Before you go, there's just one thing I've never asked you. What age are you exactly? Mr Stagg said he thought you were around thirteen or fourteen.'

'He remembers me?'

'He does. He recalls you had a lot to say about clouds.' I can hear the smile in her voice.

'I'm twelve. Thirteen next week, in fact.'

'Goodness! Well, what you did is even more extraordinary, in that case. I hope one day people will hear all about it. You're a real heroine. You saved the day finding that extra barometer.'

'That bit was my friend, Sibby,' I say. 'She's the one who really saved the day.' I think of something. 'Maureen, you know the weather reports from the last few days and nights, the ones you have in the Met Office, I mean? Is there any way you can put her name on them somewhere? I know it's a strange request and no-one will ever see it, but it would mean a lot to me and Sibby. She's my best friend, you see. I've already put her name in our ledger.'

Maureen gives a laugh. 'You are a funny one, but I'll try. What's her full name?'

'Elizabeth Lavelle,' I say. 'But everyone calls her Sibby.'

'Sibby Lavelle it is then. I'll do my best. I promise.'

'Thanks, Maureen.'

'No, thank you, Grace. For everything. It's been an honour working with you.' I hear what sounds like a sniff. 'Goodness, I've come over all teary. Sorry about that. It's been quite the time. You go off and enjoy that walk now. *Slán*, Grace.'

'*Slán*, Maureen.'

* * *

Dad and Dannie power up the hill, hot on the heels of Lucky and Poppy. Flora and I follow on behind. As we pass the entrance to the field where Hans's plane crashed, I stop at the gate and stare in. The burnt-out skeleton of the Junkers is still there.

As I study it, I think about all the young airmen like Hans and Reggie, the Germans and the Allies, the ones who made it and the ones who didn't. And those still fighting right now. It makes me sad. I blow my breath out in a whoosh.

Flora puts her arm around my shoulders. She doesn't say anything, just stands there with me, surveying the wreckage.

Up ahead of us on the hill, Poppy and Lucky are barking at a bird or a rabbit.

Flora takes my hand. 'Let's keep going, Grace,' she says. 'Make the most of our time, before we have to file another weather report.'

There are so many things swirling around in my head – the invasion, Hans and his burns, and his friends who died. Alfie. So many thoughts that I can't seem to tie one down, let alone clear my mind.

'Flora,' I say. 'This invasion. How many people will die?'

'Too many,' she says gently. 'Far, far too many. Try not to think about it, pet. The war won't go on forever. There will be peace soon, I promise. Life will go back to normal.'

'I hope so.'

Poppy and Lucky bark again. Flora brushes my hair back off my face, her hand cool against my skin. 'Right now, we are all together and we are all safe,' she says. 'And that, for now, is enough. Now, last one to the top of the hill has to do the night-time weather report!'

'Ha!' I say. 'You're on!'

I start running.

Diamond dust

A fog made up of ice crystals which glitter in the sky.
Sometimes known as ice fog. When the sun shines through
diamond dust, a halo can form

EPILOGUE

Flora was right – the war does end. On September 2nd, 1945, to be precise, more than a year on from D-Day. They say D-Day changed the direction of the war. Without it, the Allies may not have won. Of course, we couldn't tell anyone about the Blacksod weather reports or how we helped prevent the Allied troops from invading France during a storm.

A lot has happened in a year. I won that scholarship to St Mary's, the best secondary school in Castlebar. It's tough and the teachers make you work hard, but I love it. Dad has said if I keep up my studies, he'll let me study science at Trinity College in Dublin once I've done my Leaving Certificate. The same college where Flora did her Masters in Engineering. I can't wait!

Flora laughed when Dad said he'd 'let' me study science. 'Try stopping her,' she said. 'Grace is going to Trinity, if she wants to, and that's that, Tom.'

Ellen's already in Dublin, the first girl in Blacksod to study medicine at the Royal College of Surgeons. Imagine that! Everyone's so proud of her, even Sibby! And guess who's also studying in Dublin ... Hans! He's continuing his studies in Meteorology in University College Dublin. They're officially a couple now, but Ellen says she's not getting married until she's a fully qualified doctor. That will take years, but Hans says for Ellen he's happy to wait.

Sibby has set up her own theatrical company, no less, called the Blacksod Players, and they're about to present their first play in the community hall, *Peter Pan*. I suggested it to her – Alfie loved *Peter Pan*! She's letting me be the stage manager, and Dannie and Liam are two of the Lost Boys. Liam wanted to be Captain Hook, but Sibby chose Michael O'Shea instead. She told me she still has a bit of a crush on him, but she's sworn me to secrecy. And this time I know to keep my mouth shut!

Sibby and I have promised never to fall out again. On my thirteenth birthday, she gave me the best birthday present ever, a second-hand microscope that Mamó found in a junk shop in Belmullet.

'When we're old and grey we'll sit and talk about my amazing theatrical career and your weird germ discoveries,' she said, handing it over. Weird germ discoveries? Charming!

Even if Sibby and I do annoy each other sometimes, I know we'll find our way back to each other. We belong together. I know that for certain. Friends forever. Kindred spirits.

'The Irish Best Friends Who Helped Save D-Day'

Irish Independent

6th June, 2012

Papers from the World War 2 war office in Portsmouth have just been released. They relate to D-Day and Ireland's once hidden role in the weather forecasting for what was officially known as Operation Overlord.

Vital weather information which helped with the planning and the delay of the Allied invasion of France to avoid a storm came from the weather station at Blacksod, Co Mayo.

At the time, the registered lighthouse keeper was Mr Thomas Devine, also chief weather reporter. However, the names on the weather report for 6th June, 1944, D-Day, are Ms Grace Devine and Ms Sibby Lavelle.

Mr Dannie Devine retired as lighthouse keeper in 1994 and still lives in Blacksod, where he runs walking tours with his trusty dogs. When contacted, he confirmed that it was his sister Grace and her best friend Sibby who worked on the weather reports during that fateful time, along with himself and his parents, Flora and Tom Devine, both deceased.

We tracked down Grace Devine, now a spritely eighty-year-old living in Brussels, where she runs the European Climate Justice Now organisation.

She was the first 'weather girl' on RTÉ television before moving to Met Éireann, where she became the first female director. She is a regular visitor to Blacksod. When asked about the D-Day weather reports, she said:

'I still remember it, of course. You don't forget something like that. I couldn't have done it without my best friend, Sibby. Make sure to include her in your article, won't you? Sibby Lavelle. And make sure to say she's my best friend. You may know her as Elizabeth O'Shea. She's won a lot of awards for her acting, including a BAFTA. She now runs a drama school in Dublin. Being friends with Sibby has been the most important thing in my life.'

'Even more important than D-Day?' we asked her.

'To me, yes!' she said.

What a story!

HISTORICAL NOTE

The Weather Girls is a work of fiction, but it was inspired by real history and a real person. I created the Devine family from scratch, and the events in the book are fictional, but Grace's role as a 'weather girl' was inspired by real-life events and a real woman called Maureen Sweeney (née Flavin). I named the kind Irish 'weather girl' in the Met Office in Dunstable after Maureen.

In case, like me, you are a curious person and are interested in the real history that inspired this story, I put together these historical notes for you. I hope you enjoy them!

Maureen Flavin and the real D-Day weather report

Maureen Flavin was originally from Knockanure in County Kerry. She moved to Blacksod in County Mayo when she was hired as an assistant in the post office. Her additional role as a weather reporter at the weather observation station beside the post office came as a surprise to her! She was put in charge of sending the weather reports from Blacksod, which made their way to the Met Office in Dunstable, England. In the book, Grace rings Dunstable directly, but in reality this was done via Ballina and Dublin. James Stagg in the book is also inspired by a real person, also called James Stagg. He was the meteorologist who persuaded General Eisenhower, the American general who was Supreme Commander of the Allied Forces, to delay the date of D-Day based on Maureen's weather reports.

Maureen and Ted on their wedding day.

Maureen was the first person to report the incoming storm that led to the delay of D-Day. D-Day was the name given to the invasion on June 6th, 1944, of the beaches at Normandy in northern France by troops from the United States, Canada, the United Kingdom and other countries. France was under German control at this time, and the operation that began on D-Day started the liberation of western Europe from occupation. It created a chain of events that ended in Germany's surrender and the end of the Second World War.

Maureen married Ted Sweeney, the lighthouse keeper, in 1946

and eventually took over as postmistress, working there until she retired. You can watch Maureen talk about the D-Day weather reports in a short film made by her grandson, Fergus Sweeney. It is called *The Dice are on the Carpet* by Fliuch Films, and you can find it in YouTube.

Maureen passed away in 2023, aged 100. She will always be remembered as a remarkable Irish woman who helped change history.

The weather reports in *The Weather Girls*

Grace's weather reports are based on the actual weather reports from the time, given by Maureen and recorded by the UK Met Office. I changed some of the details to suit the story, but where possible I kept the figures as close as possible to the actual readings. You can check out the 1944 weather reports on their website:

https://digital.nmla.metoffice.gov.uk/collection_86058de1-8d55-4bc5-8305-5698d0bd7e13/

Blacksod Lighthouse and the Sweeney family

Blacksod Lighthouse in the book is based on the real lighthouse which was built in 1864 from local granite blocks. It has been a working lighthouse since 1866 and is also a refuelling station for search and rescue operations. It was automated in 1999.

Ted (Edward) Sweeney was appointed as the lighthouse keeper at Blacksod in 1933. Before that, the lighthouse keepers at nearby Blackrock Island used to look after it. Currently Vincent Sweeney,

Ted and Maureen's son, is the official Blacksod lighthouse keeper, and Vincent's brother, Gerry, is assistant keeper.

Blacksod Lighthouse is open to the public, so you can visit and find out all about its remarkable history. If you're very lucky, Fergus Sweeney, who is in charge of visitor experience at the lighthouse, might even be your tour guide! visitblacksodlighthouse.ie

Ireland during 'The Emergency'

In September 1939, the Irish government, Dáil Éireann, brought in new laws called the Emergency Powers Act to help them rule in time of war. After that, in Ireland, World War 2 became known as 'The Emergency'. Ireland was neutral and did not fight in the war, and most Irish people agreed with this stance. However, Ireland helped the Allies in many different ways. This included sending them regular weather reports.

The Marine and Coastwatching Service

After 1939, a network of around eighty-three lookout posts were built around the coast of Ireland. These were small stone buildings with windows facing the sea. Members of the Local Defence Force – the Marine and Coastwatching Service – recorded the ships and aircraft they could see from their lookout posts in a special logbook. This information was passed on to Irish military intelligence, who in turn passed it on to the RAF and the British Royal Navy.

You can see digital copies of these actual logbooks on the Irish Military Archives website. There are 481 logbooks in the collection, and they make fascinating reading!

https://www.militaryarchives.ie/collections/reading-room-collections/look-out-post-logbooks-september-1939-june-1945

The Éire signs

Each lookout post was numbered one to eighty-three. From the summer of 1943 onwards, the Coast Watch men were asked to build marker signs near their posts, sometimes helped by members of the local community. These were called the Éire signs or Éire markings. They were to be twelve meters long and six metres wide and creating using whitewashed stones to mark out 'Éire' – Ireland – and the number of the post. Éire 60 is at Blacksod Bay, and the one in the photograph, Éire 64, is further east along the coast at Downpatrick Head. It took around 150 tons of stone to make each sign, and they were embedded in concrete.

The signs were made to ensure that pilots knew they were flying

over neutral Irish territory (and not to bomb it). They also acted as an aid for navigation. The Allies were given details of the signs and the numbers; the Germans were not.

For more about the Coast Watching Service, see the book *Guarding Neutral Ireland* by Michael Kennedy.

Did German planes really crash in Ireland?

In a word, yes! During World War 2 around 170 planes crashed on Irish territory. Around fifty-six Luftwaffe (German air force) airmen landed during this time and were interned (imprisoned) in the Curragh prisoner of war camps.

In 1941, a Luftwaffe Condor bomber crashed on a mountain near Dunbeacon in West Cork. Local nurse Mary Nugent rushed to the scene, and she and her brother dragged the radio operator, Max Hohaus, away from the wreckage and saved his life.

For more about plane crashes during World War 2, see *Landfall Ireland: The Story of Allied and German Aircraft Which Came Down in Éire in World War Two* by Donal MacCarron.

German naval and air force officers interned at the Curragh Camp.
Photo courtesy of the Military Archives, Ireland.

The Curragh Internment Camp, County Kildare

In the book, Hans is sent to an internment camp in Kildare. This is based on a real camp. In 1940 'K-Lines' (number two internment camp) was built to intern (that is, to keep someone as a prisoner for political reasons) any Axis or Allied servicemen who were captured on Irish soil during World War 2.

It was surrounded by fourteen-foot fences and barbed wire to prevent escape. One compound in the camp was for German and Axis servicemen ('G' Camp, as most of them were German). A second compound was for Allies ('B' Camp', as most of them were British).

There was an indoor swimming pool and playing fields. Prisoners were allowed to go to the pub and the cinema, and they were well fed. Like Hans, many of the prisoners were allowed to study at colleges in Dublin, including eighteen German servicemen who studied in University College Dublin. Around four German servicemen married Irish women and stayed in Ireland – again, just like Hans!

In 1943, Ireland released the thirty-three Allied servicemen it was holding in the Curragh, while keeping the Germans in the camp. After that, Allied servicemen were secretly escorted across the border into Northern Ireland. Yet another way that Ireland helped the Allies!

Following the end of the war, around 260 German servicemen were sent back to their homeland. Many had happy memories of their time spent in Ireland and returned to visit Kildare after the war.

When did World War 2 end?

World War 2 officially ended on 2nd September, 1945. In the decades since, wars continue to happen. Countries still invade other countries, lives are lost, families are split up, and children have to move to find safety in different countries. Wars end, but they leave lasting scars. Those who live through them never forget.

ACKNOWLEDGEMENTS

This book took many years to research and write. I first became interested in the story of Maureen Flavin (Sweeney) and the Blacksod D-Day weather report when I watched a programme about lighthouses on RTÉ. I wanted to find out more about Maureen and I read all I could about the Blacksod weather reports and their impact on D-Day.

I'm especially grateful to Fergus Sweeney from Blacksod, grandson of Maureen, who kindly read this book, showed me around Blacksod Lighthouse and talked to me about his grandmother and life as a 'lighthouse family'.

I'd also like to thank Conor Sweeney (no relation to Maureen or Fergus, but what a wonderful coincidence!) for his help with the weather research and for sending me the UK Met Office information. Danke schön to Eoin Fegan for his help with the German phrases in the book.

The team at The O'Brien Press has always been incredibly supportive and helpful. Many thanks to my editor, Nicola Reddy, who carefully edited Grace and Sibby's story. Lots of other people in The O'Brien Press were involved in bringing this book to life – all of them important. Thank you to Ivan O'Brien, Managing Director, Kunak McGann, Rights Director, Publishing Assistant Rebekah Wade, Sinéad Lalor in accounts, and Kasandra Ferguson, Administrator; editors Helen Carr, Susan Houlden, Eoin O'Brien (who also drew the lovely internal illustrations) and Paula Elmore; Art Director Emma Byrne and Production Manager Bex

Sheridan (who also did our map); Brenda Boyne, Elena Browne, Gabbie Pop, Laura Feeney, Ruth Heneghan and Chloe Coome in Sales, Publicity and Marketing.

Thank you to illustrator Charli Vance for the wonderful cover and to Emma Walsh for all the PR help and advice. My agent Philippa Milnes-Smith is always there for great advice and hand-holding too.

I'd also like to thank my writer friends, especially Martina Devlin, Marita Conlon-McKenna, Judi Curtin, Alan Nolan, Patricia Forde and Eve McDonnell for listening to 1944 and lighthouse facts for years. Your patience, support and encouragement are much appreciated. Writing is a solitary job by nature and having friends who understand the highs and lows of the writing life makes it all a lot more fun.

My sisters, Kate and Emma Webb, dad Michael Webb, and life-long friends Tanya, Nicky and Andrew now know a lot more about 1944 and lighthouses than they wish to – thank you all for your collective patience!

My partner Ben also knows a LOT about Ireland during The Emergency as it became one of my favourite topics for many years, but if I was boring him, he never let on. And he genuinely loves lighthouses! Thank you for your interest in this book and all the research it took and for driving me around Mayo.

I'd like to thank Elaina Ryan and all at Children's Books Ireland for all they do for children's books in Ireland, and the amazing children's booksellers and librarians who do so much to help children find a favourite book.

The Discover Irish Children's Books team are always so

supportive, as are my fellow booksellers at Halfway up the Stairs, the wonderful Trish Hennessy, Amanda Dunne Fulmer, Kathleen Macadam and Meriel O'Toole.

And finally, I'd like to thank and cheer on all the teachers who have invited me into their classrooms all over Ireland, both in person and virtually, over the years, especially those who run their school library, like Derek Carney in St Mary's Dorset Street. I see you and I know what amazing work you do in helping to create keen young readers. Irish children deserve to read great Irish stories and you do your best to help them find them. Thank you!

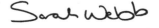